To John Wilhite,
With all best wishes.
Tom Parker

Promise
of the
faraway flower

By Tom Parks

Illustrations by Robert Ariail

Commissioned by the Park Seed Company

Copyright © 1993 by Kendall/Hunt Publishing Company

ISBN 0-8403-8780-6

Printed in the United States of America.
10 9 8 7 6 5 4 3 2 1

This book is dedicated to

George W. Park

who in 1868 at the age of 15 published and distributed his first seed catalog of 500 copies to begin a tradition of excellence in service, research and leadership that resulted in one of the world's foremost horticultural centers, the Park Seed Company, whose catalogs go annually to many millions of gardeners and others throughout the world.

Acknowledgements

Story books don't just happen. They emerge from deep sources of people and places and experiences, and the writer is only lucky to bring them to the surface. The author acknowledges with thanks the help of Mr. Fred Sheheen, Commissioner of Higher Education in South Carolina and the world's best catalyst; Mr. J. Leonard Park and Mrs. Karen Park Jennings, grandchildren of the founder of Park Seed, whose heritage embodies the best of both horticulture and humanity; Mrs. Edmee Reel and Mrs. Patsy Martin, two school librarians who exemplify the best of that noble calling; Miss Erin Wheeler of Texas, the perfect model for any book about a great kid; her parents, Gene and Gayle Wheeler; Mr. Larry Haggard, whose research and support kept everything going; Dr. Bill West and his wife Sharon, purveyors of the perfect pineapple appearing in this story; and my other colleagues on the Clemson faculty, Dr. Shelley Barbary, Dr. Carolyn Briscoe, and Dr. Bea Cain.

The publication of this book is commissioned by Park Seed Company of Greenwood, South Carolina, to commemorate the 125th anniversary of its founding in 1868. Proceeds from sales of the book will go to a scholarship fund for minority students administered by the South Carolina Commission on Higher Education.

Rain Forest Meets Outer Space

Horace was sick. He seemed listless and tired, totally without energy or his usual perkiness. He slouched there, next to the window, limp. Erin could almost hear him sigh.

"What on earth is wrong with you this morning?" she asked, crossing her arms and gazing at him with a curious frown that only an eleven-year old girl could muster.

Maybe too much food, she mused. *Or too much to drink. Or not enough. Or maybe too much sun. . . .* It could be anything. Her eyes, dark and intelligent, narrowed as she studied him. Gently, she reached out and placed the back of her fingers against him, as if taking his temperature. He felt cool to her touch, and weak—a patient clearly in need of care.

"Don't you worry, old friend," Nurse Erin said to him in a quiet, reassuring voice. "When I get back from school today, we will find your problem and get you back on the road to health. I promise."

She looked around the room. It was filled with plants—plants of all kinds, plants that festooned the windows and every shelf space and table with a thousand shades of green. It was a big sunlit room with windows on three sides, and all the different plants that burst forth from every nook and cranny made it seemed to Erin like a frothing green sea.

She loved the plants, every one of them, and Horace was one of her very favorites. He was a Dieffenbachia. Erin felt sure that he had been a member of the family longer than she had. She could barely remember when her parents divorced several years ago, but Horace had been around even then and had moved with Erin and her mother to this condominium on the edge of town. It was a nice place with this big, bright room which her mother called "the sun room." It soon became Erin's favorite room, and she filled it with the plants she had come to love over the years.

"I want all of you to look after Horace today while I'm gone," she announced to the plants in the room. "Here, Priscilla, you can keep a close eye on him," she whispered to a

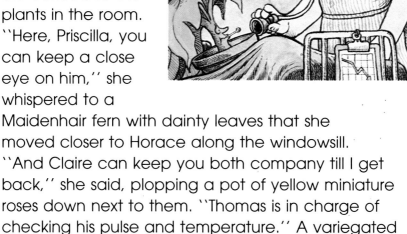

Maidenhair fern with dainty leaves that she moved closer to Horace along the windowsill. "And Claire can keep you both company till I get back," she said, plopping a pot of yellow miniature roses down next to them. "Thomas is in charge of checking his pulse and temperature." A variegated ivy vine was gently placed alongside the ailing Horace.

"And what's wrong with Horace this morning?" Erin's mother asked, leaning in the doorway and sipping coffee. "Is he the one with the yellow leaves?"

2

Erin rolled her éyes and smiled to herself.

"No, Mom. That's Clementine. She's *supposed* to have yellow leaves. Horace is this one, with the big, shiny green leaves. Except they're not so shiny now. And see how limp they are? He's sick."

"Well, I hope he can hold out, because we have to leave now or you'll be late for school," her mother said, rinsing her coffee cup and turning it upside down in the kitchen sink. Mrs. Beddingfield was a tall woman. She dressed in high heels and a business suit that let people know she meant business, and she had a way of tilting her head back and looking through the bottom part of her glasses at anybody who doubted it. Very few doubted it. Her office was on the top floor of a tall bank building downtown, where Erin sometimes visited to see the view.

Her mother knew a lot about business, but Erin knew she didn't know anything about plants. But that was fine. She sometimes laughed at her mother for not knowing the difference between Clementine and Horace, and sometimes her mother laughed at Erin for all the time and attention she gave to her plants.

"One of these days, Kiddo, you've got to stop talking to plants and start talking to people," her mother had said once. It had been an off-hand remark that she hoped wouldn't sound too serious. But Erin blushed; she thought it may be true. Was she crazy because she liked plants so much? She didn't think so. After all, they were living things, too, and they were so kind and patient and beautiful. At least they weren't imaginary playmates like some of her little friends once had. As for people—well, she didn't really *dislike* her classmates in sixth grade, it was just that . . . right now she liked her plants more. There was something about them that had always fascinated her above all else. Her teacher this year, Miss Barbary, had called her ``our future botanist'' one day in front of the whole class, and Erin did her usual trick: she blushed. She just hated being shy, especially when people reminded her of it.

Just in time for the final bell that morning, Erin slid into her seat. She sat in the third desk in the last row next to the window. From there, on the days when she finished her work early, she could gaze out the window and try to catalog all the different trees and shrubs. On breezy days, the leaves of the big silver maple on the corner shimmered in a delicate kind of rhythm that seemed like silent music. And like the world's slowest clock, the huge feathery leaves on the giant sycamore turned from deep green in summer to gold and yellow and

brown in the fall, then slowly started cascading down, marking the world's time. *Tick* . . . Erin said silently to herself this morning as she noticed the first leaf fall. And then *tock*. . . . as the next one fell. She smiled. The world's clockwork.

Then she looked up and discovered Miss Barbary frowning at her from the front of the room. *Blush.* She had been caught daydreaming and now felt the heat of what the sixth graders had secretly termed the Silent Scold. It was Miss Barbary's specialty. She was a good teacher, but she did not allow any signs of drifting into daydreams. The dreaded Silent Scold came when her voice dropped a couple of octaves, she paused in what she was saying, and her eyes pierced the silence like a laser beam aimed at the drifter.

Erin had received the dreaded Silent Scold first thing this morning. Then Miss Barbary went on with what she was saying. Had anybody seen? She looked around, studying the faces row by row. Maybe nobody saw, and she wouldn't be teased at recess.

Except. Oh, no. Of all people. Will Moreland. As usual, there he was, sitting on the front row, never missing a thing that went on in the classroom. Erin sometimes thought Will had eyes in the back of his head. He had certainly had more than his share of Silent Scolds; but it never seemed to bother him. In fact, he seemed to enjoy the teasing he got later—unlike Erin, who always blushed, said nothing, and hated herself for blushing.

Anybody but Will Moreland, Erin thought. *Now I'll never hear the end of it.*

Will was class president, and some of the girls

thought he was cute. But Erin just thought he was silly, with his crazy excitement about outer space. That's all he ever seemed to think about: outer space, outer space, outer space.

"Today, class, we're going to wrap up our unit on rain forests," Miss Barbary said, "and then I've got an important announcement to make. Right now, turn to page 88."

Erin remembered most of the facts in the review from the first time they had studied them, but she was still interested because the rain forests were as much about plants as anything. But she was alone in her fascination, because everybody else in class was just coasting along, wondering what in the wide world Miss Barbary's important announcement could be.

"Remember, about 15 percent of the earth's land surface was covered by rain forests for thousands of years, class," the teacher droned on. "But within the last 200 years, over half that area has been converted into wasteland or open fields. Isn't that a tragedy?"

They murmured and nodded their heads and thought *oh yes, it is, whatever you say, Miss Barbary, but would you just get on with your important announcement?*

"Furthermore, every year, 10 to 20 million acres are completely destroyed. Which means. . . ." She paused and leaned over her desk. Her fingers did a staccato dance over the keys of her little calculator. No doubt about it: the purveyor of the Silent Scold was fast. "Which means," she continued, "that around forty acres disappear somewhere in the world every minute of every day. Between now and recess, that would be . . . let's see, that would be over one thousand acres of rain forest in the next 24 minutes. Can you imagine that, class?''

Right, right, right. Their collective thoughts bounced like silent ping pong balls around the room. *So what's the important announcement?*

''And one animal species becomes extinct every one-half hour. Now, who can tell me what the term *transpiration* means?''

Silence. Nobody raised a hand.

''Don't you remember? It was on the list of new vocabulary words I gave you for this unit on the rain forest,'' Miss Barbary said in an even voice that hinted that a huge, communal Silent Scold might be on the way.

Ralph Sims raised his hand. He never knew anything. The whole class was amazed. *Get us off the hook, Ralph,* they thought in unison.

''It's how you go from one place to another, like on a bus,'' he said.

''No, that's trans*por*tation, Ralph. Close, but I want trans*pir*ation.'' She looked around. Everybody froze and avoided looking at her.

''Erin Beddingfield, I'll bet you remember. You're our botanist.''

Erin blushed and scoonched down in her desk. Out of the corner of her eye she saw Will Moreland's hand waving in the air.

''It's when plants breathe vapor through their leaves,'' she said quickly, sitting up straight.

''Exactly,'' Miss Barbary said.

There, Will Moreland, Erin thought. *You stick to your science fiction and I'll stick to my science facts.*

She settled back down in her desk and forgot that she wasn't blushing anymore. She and Will were the two top science students in the sixth grade. They always made the highest grades. However, that was about all they seemed to have in common. Will belonged in outer space; that's all he ever talked about. *Worse than a fifth grader sometimes,* Erin thought. And as for herself . . . well, she belonged right here on earth, with her plants. She wondered how Horace was doing.

"The huge trees in the rain forest draw up lots of water from their roots, then release it as vapor though their leaves. From there, it condenses into clouds in the atmosphere and falls again as rain," Miss Barbary was saying. "So rain forests help regulate the earth's climatic conditions, especially rainfall. Remember transpiration; it will be on the test."

A low groan arose from the class. *Don't talk tests at a time like this. Now can we get on with it?* they wondered. *C'mon. Give us the important announcement.*

"In the few minutes we have left, I want to remind you about the Science Fair," Miss Barbary said. "Don't forget that every one of you must have a project. Each and every one. We've studied the scientific principles and know how to conduct experiments. That's what your Science Fair project will have to be. Tomorrow I'll hand out directions, and we'll talk about the rules and regulations. But today I want you to start thinking about your project. Any questions?"

Will's hand shot up. "What's the important announcement you had for us?" he asked.

"That was it. The Science Fair," she said.

Shoulders slumped in the ensuing silence. That was it? They had sat through the destruction of the rain forests for that?

8

"It's very important," Miss Barbary said. "The winner at our school goes to the district competition and then to the state capital and on to the national in Washington."

Suddenly, without warning, there was a loud crash in the hallway right outside the classroom door. Everybody jumped, including Miss Barbary.

"What on earth was that?" she exclaimed, and rushed to open the door. The students craned their necks to see.

It was Mrs. Oglethorp. She was the school librarian, known among the students as the Lady of the Consequences. She always talked of consequences.

The overloaded, rickety book cart which she had been pushing, with its one wobbly wheel and three squeaking ones, had finally collapsed from the weight and emptied half its contents at the doorway.

"I am so very, very sorry," Mrs. Oglethorp said, piling the scattered books randomly back onto the cart. "That's the consequence of having too much Dewey Decimal on this poor old cart." She wobbled it into the classroom and then sat down primly in a nearby chair, like someone waiting to go on stage. Mrs. Oglethorp always wore print dresses with little flowers on them, a white belt, and white shoes. Always. And smelled like flowers.

Skitzy is what Will Moreland had called her once. They were in line waiting to check out library books, and they had watched Mrs. Oglethorp drop the date stamp three times. But he meant no harm, whatever *skitzy* meant. Everybody liked the librarian, even if she was . . . well, skitzy sometimes. And they liked her husband Frank even more. He owned the hardware store in town but spent most of his time at the school.

He worked on shelves, added partitions, and repaired library tables and chairs or whatever else Mrs. Oglethorp and the teachers asked him to. He always wore khaki pants, black shoes, and blue short-sleeve shirts.

Once, Mrs. Oglethorp interrupted the silence of the library to announce, ``Boys and girls. We'll have to disturb your silent reading for just a minute while Mr. Oglethorp nails a little piece of wood to this table. It won't take long. Now, let's all place our hands over our ears for protection against the noise because we know the consequences of loud noise to our hearing.'' They all dutifully did so, but only for a second, because Mr. Oglethorp hit his thumb with the hammer and made lots more interesting noise than any nailing they'd ever heard.

``Yeeoowww!'' he yelled, slinging his hand sharply back and forth.

``Boys and girls. Boys and girls!'' Mrs. Oglethorp said quickly, ``Cover your ears!'' as her husband did a little dance around the library table, holding his throbbing thumb. ``Quickly, now, let's all cover our ears!''

But it was too late. They still heard a couple of Mr. Oglethorp's strong words that they knew he just couldn't help. That day was one of the few times that Mrs. Oglethorp was totally unable to keep everybody settled down and not giggling among themselves in the library, whatever the consequences.

But today she had brought samples of library books about all kinds of science to help the students choose a project for the Science Fair. She held up one after another: insects, mammals, crustaceans, microbes, whales, diseases, chemistry, plants, colors, seasons, birds, clouds, earthquakes, the solar system. . . .

"Everybody ought to choose outer space because there's room enough for all the science projects in the world," Will burst out when she mentioned the solar system.

"Will Moreland, be quiet and let me finish or face the consequences," Mrs. Oglethorp said. "It's almost time for the bell." She reached for the next book on the stack.

"Oh, here's a good one, boys and girls. I know you just finished a unit on the rain forests, and this is about what's happening. . . ." her voice dropped as she riffled through the pages. Then she stopped and laid it limply on the cart and sort of shook her head slowly.

"So sad. So very, very sad," she said, stepping to the side of the room and leaning ever so slightly against the wall before she went on. "You see, I have a dear, dear niece who suffers terribly from asthma. And do you know, they think they may have found a plant in the tropics that can help cure it, but now they're afraid the forests are being destroyed where it grows. We can only hope," she sighed, barely above a whisper as she raised a frilly handkerchief to her bosom and added the slightest hint of a quiver to her voice, "that it's not too late."

The room was very silent. Erin could feel a small lump in her throat and thought she may have heard a few sniffles here and there from some of the girls in the room.

Brrrinnngg! The bell brought the class back to life, and the students exploded onto the schoolyard for recess. Erin found herself at the edge of a small group

11

of girls wondering about what project they might come up with for the Science Fair, when up popped Will Moreland.

"MagNIFicent!" he exclaimed using his favorite word. "Did you hear Ogie in there? What a performance! MagNIFicent!" and he jabbed the air in front of him with his fist in a swift uppercut.

"What?" the girls asked in unison. "Who?"

"Ogie. You know. Mrs. Oglethorp. What an act. She was great! Can you believe that performance?" He leaned to one side and placed the back of his hand over his forehead. "Oh, oh, oh. So, so sad. If only we're . . . (gulp) . . . not too late," and he crumpled to the ground.

"Will Moreland!" Erin said suddenly, stamping her foot and astonishing herself. "Mrs. Oglethorp was serious! And it's not funny. What she said was true!"

The other girls stared at her. Their mouths practically hung open with surprise. This was Erin? This was the shy girl who sat by the window and almost never said anything, who blushed every time somebody looked at her?

"Yeah, right," Will said, getting up from his fake faint and brushing off the dust. "If there's a cure for asthma, you can bet it'll come from space medicine of some kind—not some witch doctor's hokey flower somewhere in the jungle." And with that, he started sauntering away, his head held high in a superior way that Erin could not stand.

"Half the medicines in the world come from rain forests," she called after him. "How many come from *outer space?*" and she really gave a good twist to the last two words. The other girls jumped in their tracks and applauded.

"Oh, Erin," they chimed in together. "That was wonderful. You put him in his place. And we thought you were shy!"

Erin was even more surprised at herself than they were. Why on earth had she acted so . . . well, different from usual? Maybe she wasn't shy after all.

"By the way, Erin," Will called back over his shoulder without stopping his walk. "I saw the Barb give you the SS this morning for looking out the window. Where was your mind—in outer space? Ha-ha-ha!" Then he ran away.

And in spite of all, Erin did the one thing she hoped that she would never do again. She blushed. The other girls looked at their new leader and giggled.

Is the Space Salad Ready?

Erin sat at the kitchen table with her head in her hands, staring straight ahead.

"Eat your cereal, Kiddo, or you won't grow up to be big and strong like your Mom," her mother said.

"Oh, Mom. I just can't decide. It's not the easiest thing in the world, you know," Erin said, mouthing a spoonful of soggy cereal.

"Sure it is. It's simple. For your Science Fair project, you just make a poster," and she blocked out the wording on an imaginary poster in the air in front of her. "And you say, 'Here's the problem with Horace. Here are his symptoms, and here's what I did to cure him.' Then, you have Horace there in all his glory, healthy and shining. And *Presto!* There's your project, signed, sealed, and delivered, with all the right scientific principles. It's as easy as pie."

"Oh, no—I just couldn't do that. It's not enough," Erin said, frowning and shaking her head. "Besides, I'm worried. Horace is not cured yet, and I can't figure out what's wrong with him."

"What?" her mother asked in false alarm, placing her hand to her chest in mock horror. "Do you mean to tell me that My Daughter the Mad Scientist has actually met a plant she can't control?"

Erin laughed and threw a paper napkin at her mom.

"Seriously, Mom," she said. "I've checked everything. Food, light, water, insects, disease. Nothing. I've come up with nothing. Horace is in serious trouble. Really."

Her mother got up and took her coffee cup with her into the sun room.

"I know. I really didn't mean to sound so unconcerned. But you'll find a cure for Horace—whatever he is and whichever he is," she said, looking around in genuine confusion at all the plants. "I know you will."

"Besides," Erin said, her voice taking on a tone of determination. "I want to come up with a project better than Will Moreland's. I just know he'll have some kind of cool outer space project with all kinds of special effects and gimmicks, and I've got to beat him."

"Well, well, well," her mother said, pouring another cup of coffee and sitting back down at the kitchen table. "Is that the Moreland boy, Jesse and Maxine Moreland's son?" She slurped her coffee.

Erin placed both hands under her chin. "I guess so. I think his dad owns an insurance company and his mother is on some kind of commission or something. I'm not sure."

"Yes, of course," her mother said. "A wonderful couple. I hear he's a fine young man."

Oh, Mother! Erin thought, squinching her eyes tight. *How can adults be so crazy?*

"Well, he's not. Not at all," Erin replied, scraping her spoon in the bowl for the last soggy cereal. "Will Moreland is . . . he's just a pest," she said; and, in spite of all, found herself blushing. "All he thinks about is outer space, and he thinks he knows everything. But he doesn't."

"Good," her mother said, and Erin thought she detected the slightest smile on her mother's face. "Because I know you can come up with a better project than he can, as much as you know about plants.'' She walked back into the sun room, sipping her coffee. ''Horace, wherever you are and whichever you are,'' she announced, holding up her coffee cup, ''here's to your health.''

Oh, Mom, Erin thought, shaking her head and smiling at her mother. *You wouldn't know Horace if he had his name stamped on every leaf and started tap-dancing this very minute.*

''Yuck. I am drinking too much coffee,'' her mother said suddenly. ''Got to cut down. Okay, Kiddo. Time to go; the day is calling.''

Erin tucked her problem about Horace and her problem about the Science Fair project into her backpack like little black clouds and headed down the street to school. The problems seemed to be getting bigger by the day, taking up more and more room in her thoughts.

At school, Miss Barbary didn't have to give a single Silent Scold all day, although she came close when she handed back the test papers on the Rain Forests. Will's hand shot up.

''I can't believe I missed the last question, Miss Barbary,'' he said. ''Wasn't the right answer **d. ten percent?** It was the only one I missed. Maybe you made a mistake.''

Just for a second, Erin thought she saw the hint of an SS appear on the Barb's face like a tiny ripple across the surface of still waters. But then it was gone.

''Who can help Will with the right answer?'' Miss Barbary asked, looking around the room. ''Let me read the question. *Approximately what percentage of the world's plant and animal species make their home in tropical forests?''*

Erin was surprised to look up and find several of the other students looking at her. Then, to make it clear that they expected her to answer, Ralph Sims said to nobody in particular, "Erin made a hundred on the test."

"Yes, I know, Ralph. Thank you for telling us. Erin, what's the correct answer?" Miss Barbary asked.

"It's **b. fifty percent,**" Erin said, and she was aware that she had not blushed at all and had not even scoonched down in her seat.

"Wow! Fifty percent?" Will said, incredulous that his answer wasn't even close. "I don't know where my mind was—in outer space, I guess."

"Earth calling Will. Earth calling Will," Ralph Sims said, with his hands cupped around his mouth like a loudspeaker. Everybody in class laughed, including Miss Barbary and even, Erin noticed, Will, too.

"Enough of this," Miss Barbary said. "Turn in your test papers so I can file them. Now I want to check on how far along you are on your Science Fair projects."

She went down each row, calling on each student in turn and jotting down notes at their answers.

"And may I assume that yours will be about outer space?" she asked when she got to Will.

"Bigger than that. The whole solar system!" Will exclaimed, so excited that he was soon standing on his knees in his desk. "It will show where Earth fits into the whole universe in deep space, with all the other planets, even the moon. It's going to be magNIFicent!" he practically yelled, punching the air in front of him with his fist. Then he slid back down in his desk and added, "But there's still a technical difficulty or two that I have to work out. I can't divulge all the details yet, but it's going to be magNIFicent!"

"I'm sure it will be," Miss Barbary smiled, and went on to the next student. Several said they hadn't chosen a project yet.

"Now, class, don't wait too late to make your decision," she reminded them. "Good projects take a lot of time and a lot of work. If you wait too long, your project will look hurried and rushed and won't be very good. So get your thinking caps on. I want some very good projects from you."

She continued down the rows. Erin sat at her desk in a nervous fidget. What was she going to do? She didn't have the slightest idea of what her Science Fair project might be, and it would soon be her turn. Slowly but surely, Miss Barbary continued desk by desk and row by row, jotting down the great variety of projects which the students described. Some she questioned in detail before she gave final approval, but mostly she seemed pleased—at least for those who could discuss their idea for a project. Erin couldn't.

She sat there, trying to think of something and at the same time keeping an eye on Will Moreland. As usual, he was turned around in his seat, listening to what the others were planning. Erin could tell he was listening mostly to see if anybody came up with an idea that might be competition for his outer space project. So far, she could tell, nobody had.

She just had to come up with something great. She just had to.

Miss Barbary had now moved over to the last row, the one next to the window. Erin's desk was third.

Erin glanced at the big clock over the blackboard. Under it Miss Barbary had written *Time will pass. Will you?* She couldn't believe her eyes. Had that much time already passed? It was only three minutes to the bell.

Please, please, she said softly to herself. *Come on, clock. Rush it up.*

Miss Barbary called on Nancy Bazemore, who sat right in front of Erin.

Talk, Nancy, talk, Erin pleaded silently. *Talk a long time about a very complicated science project you've selected. Go into great detail. Filibuster.*

"I'm sorry, Miss Barbary," Nancy Bazemore said. "But I haven't chosen a project yet."

"Okay," Miss Barbary said, "but let me again remind those of you who don't have a project yet that time will fly by before you know it, so don't wait too long."

Then, in spite of Miss Barbary's promise that time could fly, it stood still instead. She called on Erin.

"Erin, what project have you chosen? May we assume it will be about plants?" she asked, smiling.

Bbbrriinnnggg! Saved by the bell! Erin had never felt so relieved as she and the other students started gathering up their books.

"No, no! Keep your seats for a minute, class. Let's hear what Erin has chosen," Miss Barbary said, shushing them like a flock of birds whose burst of flight had been interrupted.

"I . . . uh . . . it will be about gardening," Erin said quickly, surprised that she didn't sound half as desperate as she felt. Then, out of the blue, she remembered Mr. Oglethorp telling her about a new item he had seen advertised in a seed catalog the last time she had visited his hardware store to buy a hand trowel.

"For my project," she blurted out suddenly, "I'm thinking about growing a plant that has tomatoes on the top and potatoes on the bottom. Maybe several of them, with a chart explaining how it's done."

Erin could tell that some of the other students were intrigued by the idea of such a plant.

But not Miss Barbary.

"Yes, I have seen those plants in seed catalogs," she said, without a great deal of enthusiasm, Erin felt. "That might be interesting. Class, have any of you seen those plants?"

Erin was glad no one raised a hand. Except Ralph Sims.

"Miss Barbary," he asked. "Would it be called a pomato or a topato?"

Everyone laughed, and Will cupped his hands over his mouth and broadcast, "Earth to Erin. Earth to Erin. Is the space salad ready yet?"

This time the laughter was even louder, and Miss Barbary dismissed them with a wave of her hand and a rolling of her eyes.

"See you tomorrow," she said.

Erin quickly gathered her books, stuffed them into her backpack, and rushed out of the classroom. She didn't want to talk with anybody. She had too many questions on her mind that needed too many answers. And she knew that both the questions and the answers would have to come from within herself. She was confused, but more than anything, she was perplexed at herself. Why on earth did she just make up something out of the blue and tell Miss Barbary? Why couldn't she just have told the truth? Was it because she felt the other students expected something great from her? After all, she was the ``future botanist'' in class, and she had made 100 on the test. And had she made up an answer just because she knew Will Moreland would be watching and listening? What difference did it make if he had? she asked herself. But no answer came.

She hurried along the sidewalk until she was out of sight of the school. She wanted time to herself, time to think. It seemed she was heading from one problem at school to another one at home—from not knowing what to choose for a Science Fair project to not knowing what to do about Horace.

The sidewalk in front of her was filled with leaves— leaves of all kinds: some that reminded her of little scalloped brown sleighs from the tall pin-oaks, big bronze kites that drifted lazily from the heights of the sycamore, fluttery bunches of frilly yellow lace from the chinaberry trees here and there, mulberry leaves like tiny tan handkerchiefs. She shuffled her feet through the leaves, enjoying their autumn earth colors. They billowed up around her in splashes of red and yellow and gold and brown. *This street has a good balance,* she thought to herself, shuffling along the sea of leaves. *People need oxygen so they can breathe out carbon dioxide, and trees need carbon dioxide so they can breathe out oxygen.* She took a deep breath and felt as much a part of the trees' world as they were of hers.

She wondered: do people have seasons, too, like the trees? Surely they must; all living things must have seasons, just like plants. She smiled as she imagined the seasons of people: in the fall, their hair would change colors and fall out, like the leaves all around her; and in the spring, it would grow back, and then it would have to be cut like grass in the summer. It was funny to picture Will and Miss Barbary and Ralph Sims and everybody else in class, sitting there bald during the winter, waiting for their hair to grow out in the spring.

She smiled to herself and trudged on, kicking her way through the leaves and wondering what to do for a Science Fair project and what to do about Horace. The two problems followed her along the sidewalk like two little black clouds floating above her head amid the cascading leaves.

As Erin rounded the corner, she stopped and peered. A new car was in the driveway, parked behind her mother's. She walked up and studied it. On the back bumper was a rental car sticker.

Could it be? She brightened with hope as she hurried to the front door. There, tied on the front doorknob was a big polka-dot ribbon, and the two little clouds of worry disappeared. It could mean only one thing.

Uncle Bub was here!

Message in a Muddy Shirt

"What's going on, Kiddo?" Uncle Bub shouted, grabbing Erin in a big bear hug and spinning her round and round in the living room, with her feet flying. Uncle Bub was the one who had started calling her *Kiddo*, and Erin's mom had picked it up from him. He was her mom's younger brother, and he had always been Erin's very best pal, even though he was years older.

"You two calm down and stop knocking furniture around," her mom said, as they collapsed laughing on the sofa next to her. Uncle Bub's real name was David. But when he was younger he had been called "Bubba," a nickname for Brother, by Erin's mother. It was a name he didn't like. "Call me Uncle David. I am not Uncle Bubba," he had said when Erin was little and learning to talk. So, with much giggling, Erin and her mother always called him Uncle Bub, and that became his name.

"Where have you been this time?" Erin asked, kicking off her shoes and curling her feet beneath her on the sofa. She loved to hear Uncle Bub tell about his travels. He was a flight crew member for an airline, and his work took him all over the world. Wherever he went, he always brought Erin a souvenir and some wonderful stories about the people and the places he had seen.

"Oh, no! Another tall tale," her mother said. "I'm going to start dinner while the two of you are jabbering away. I'll listen from the kitchen." She walked to the front door, untied the the big polka-dot ribbon, and took it back to Erin's room. "Till next time," she said. Uncle Bub had used it on one of Erin's very first souvenirs, a panda doll from China, and she had saved it.

"You will not believe it this time, Kiddo," Uncle Bub said. "It was a real adventure. Do you know where Belize is?"

Erin thought for a moment. Belize. Belize. It sounded familiar. Then she remembered. Miss Barbary had talked about Belize during the unit on the rain forests. And she pronounced it "Be-leeze" just like Uncle Bub.

"I think . . . is it a country in Central America?" Erin said, and added, "Where the rain forests are?"

"Yes! That's right!" Uncle Bub said, slapping his hands together. "The first country south of Mexico. And I got to take a trip deep into the rain forest away from the cities and far into the interior of the country. It was magNIFicent!"

Oh, no, Erin thought. *He says that word exactly like Will Moreland.*

"First, to get to the interior, I got on a small single-engine airplane, not much bigger than this sofa, and the pilot took me miles and miles inland, far away from any signs of civilization," he said. "I wanted to see the real rain forests, the way they've always been for millions of years, untouched. They're cutting them down, you know."

"Yes, we studied about that," Erin answered quickly, excited by the story he was telling. "Miss Barbary, our teacher, said about ten million acres a year are being cut." She shifted her position, getting comfortable on the sofa. She loved Uncle Bub's stories of his travels, and this was turning out to be one of the best. The rain forests, from up close!

"Then this Miss Barbary is a very, very good teacher," he said. "And she's right. I wanted to see the real thing—and, boy, did I ever! I got the scare of a lifetime!''

"What happened?'' Erin asked.

"Well, when we finally landed at a little clearing in the trees, I got on a rickety old bus going to a remote village several hours away. The road was just wide enough for the bus, and it wandered about in every direction—around huge trees, down into little valleys, over hills, across streams, under huge fallen tree trunks. How we made it in that dilapidated bus I'll never know. It didn't have any doors or windows—just two open sides with a couple of long wooden benches to sit on.'' Then he paused. "But you can't believe how beautiful the forest scenery was,'' he said. "It was like a perpetual green twilight. The trees were so big and tall that their leaves overhead made it seem like we were in a great tent that covered miles and miles. It was mid-morning by then, but there was just enough sunlight filtering down to give everything this air of green magic. I may as well have been on another planet. MagNIFicent! I took lots of photos, and I'll show you the slides. They turned out great.''

"Not until after dinner!'' Erin's mother called from the kitchen.

"And then everything changed,'' Uncle Bub continued in a lower, more serious voice. "The bus suddenly drove out from under the rain forest and onto this huge, open area where all the trees had been cut down and burned away. Practically nothing was growing on it for miles and miles—almost as far as you could see. Just bare hills and gullies with piled up debris. And we'd been traveling in the soft green world for so long that the sun almost blinded us. It was so different—like two different worlds.''

Erin shifted her position again on the sofa. "But what happened? You said an awful thing happened."

"Well, the worst thing was that so many miles and miles of rain forest had been destroyed for lumber or to make pasture for cattle. But it caused the accident to happen," he continued. "In the rain forest, you know, it rains every day. Well, on our trip back from the village, it started raining, and it rained and rained and rained. The other people on the bus weren't bothered because it rained that way there every day. We were going through the open area where the land had been cleared away, and without the trees and forest floor to soak up the water, the rain just gushed away in streams and gullies in every direction. At the bottom of a little hill, the water was rushing over the road, and the driver couldn't stop in time. So the bus slid down a muddy embankment and almost turned over! And it didn't have any doors or windows, so we could have been killed. It gave us all a scare, but nobody was hurt, thank goodness. But then the water started rising and gushing into the bus, so we had to get off and try pushing it back up the embankment to the road. We kept slipping and sliding in the mud, and I fell down several times, with the rain and water gushing around me. But we finally got the bus back on the road and took off. We were all totally soaked and covered with mud and debris, but we made it."

Then Uncle Bub cocked his head to one side and gazed into the distance.

"But you know what?" he asked, contemplating. "A strange thing happened. The seven or eight other people on the bus were natives, and we couldn't understand a word each other said. But when we got back on the bus, all soaked and tired and muddy, we looked at each other and laughed and laughed. It really had a happy ending, I guess, but it was sad to see what was happening to the rain forests.''

There was silence for a moment when he finished. Erin and her mother in the kitchen had enjoyed his adventure and shared his worry about the rain forest.

''Say, I almost forgot!'' Uncle Bub said suddenly, snapping his finger and jumping up from the sofa. ''A little souvenir from the rain forest, Kiddo.'' He went into the guest room, and Erin could hear his big suitcase snapping open. She looked at her mother and ducked her head and smiled. Soon he came back holding a piece of strange material and gave it to Erin.

''I got it in the little remote village in the rain forest. It's made of leaves and flower petals, and nobody knows how they do it. But the leaves and petals don't fade or get dry and brittle.''

''It's beautiful,'' Erin said, unfolding the soft material. It was a patchwork of vibrant colors that reminded her of the stained glass windows at church. ''Mom, come look,'' she said, holding it up. ''Thanks, Uncle Bub. I've never seen anything like this.''

Erin's mother came in from the kitchen, drying her hands on a dish towel. ''How very unusual,'' she said, draping the soft material over her arm. ''And absolutely beautiful. How on earth do they make this?''

''Nobody knows,'' Uncle Bub shrugged. ''It's a secret that they won't tell. And now the small tribe who make it are being dispersed because their homeland in the rain forest is scheduled for cutting by lumber companies. So we may never know.''

''Thank you, Uncle Bub,'' Erin said, holding the fabric up to her face. She thought she could smell the slightest trace of a wonderful scent, as if the flower petals woven in the fabric were bringing her a distant message from a magic green world where they had once lived but would see no more. "It's going to be one of my favorite souvenirs."

"Yes, it is a work of art," Erin's mother said. "Now, you two wash up, and let's have dinner. It's almost ready."

"Oh, no!" Uncle Bub said suddenly, slapping his forehead. "I almost forgot to tell you. Because I was so late getting back to the airport after the muddy trip to the rain forest, I just had time to cram all my wet clothes into an extra suitcase, and I haven't had a chance to wash them."

"Do you mean to tell me that those rain forest clothes are still packed away with all their muck and debris right here in this house?" Erin's mother asked, hands on hips in a half-serious, half-joking way.

"I promise I'll clean them up right after dinner," Uncle Bub said, laughing and heading for the kitchen. "Besides, that was only two days ago, so they probably aren't that bad."

"Yuck," her mother said. "I'll bet tarantulas and boa constrictors are probably mixed in with them. You are still my little brother, and I don't trust you. Remember how you used to frighten me with spiders and snakes?" she said, laughing, as they sat down to eat.

After dinner, her mother shoo'd Erin and Uncle Bub into the living room to watch the slides.

"I'll see them another time," she said. "Right now, I want to do what I can to save those muddy clothes of yours. I don't want my washer and dryer ruined, so I'll do it myself. Now, shoo!"

30

In the living room, Uncle Bub set up his projector
and used the white wall for a screen. Erin sat back
and watched scene after scene of color photos of the
rain forest trip. He was right: it was a beautiful green
world, with splashes of bright color when an exotic bird
or glowing flower appeared in sharp contrast against
the soft dark green of the forest. She watched
entranced as he recounted his trip. It was all there: the
small plane, many photos from the air of the dense
forest below, then the rickety old bus with open sides
and no doors, and many breathtaking views of the
forest itself, alive with plants and animals of every hue
and shape, followed by many drab and colorless
views of the vast areas where the forest had been
cleared away, with the gullies and rushing streams of
muddy water. She felt she had been there herself.

"What on earth is this?" they heard her mother exclaim from the laundry room.

"Uh, oh," Uncle Bub said. "I may be in trouble. Maybe she *did* find a tarantula mixed in with my muddy clothes." Her mother came in and pitched something to Uncle Bub. It was the size of a pecan. He turned it over in his hand, studying it.

"I have the same question," he said. "What on earth is it? And where did it come from?"

"I found it stuck in the shirt pocket of your muddy clothes. Don't ask me," she said.

"Here, Erin. Take a look. You're the botanist in the family," Uncle Bub said, pitching it to Erin. "Looks like a seed of some kind. I've never seen it before. It must have washed into my pocket while I was slipping and falling in all that mud and water trying to help push the bus out of the ditch."

Erin looked at what was in her hand.

It was a seed, all right, but it was the most unusual seed she had ever seen. In some ways it was like a tiny ball of thin green thread, but then

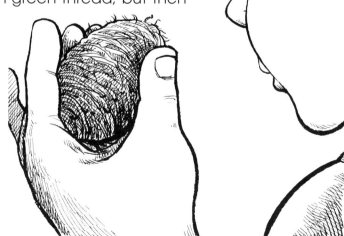

there were spaces where the kernel gleamed from underneath, almost iridescent, refracting a rainbow of soft colors. Parts of it were smooth, almost metallic, while other sections were ridged and rough, hidden by the tightly-wound fragile green threads.

''Don't look now, but I think your niece is under a spell,'' Erin's mother said to Uncle Bub.

''I'm not surprised,'' he answered, smiling at Erin. ''After all, it has to do with plants, you know.''

Erin scarcely heard either one of them. She was fascinated by the exotic seed in her hand. She turned it over and over, studying every little part of it.

What strange and wonderful place did you come from? she wondered. The rainbow of iridescent colors seemed to glow and change as she turned the seed in her hand. She tried to picture the place where it had grown: a green and balmy world far away, filled with mists and mountains and hidden glades, with ferns folding their lacy fronds to shield strange and exotic plants in secret gardens high on the hills and deep in the valleys, beneath the quiet canopy of the rain forest—an enchanted land where birds with bright plumage sang mysterious melodies, and plants with luminous leaves burst forth in clarions of color.

Never had she seen such a seed before or imagined a more magical land for plants to grow.

She looked up and found her mother and Uncle Bub smiling at her. They knew. Even before she said it, they knew.

''I have found my Science Fair project,'' she said quietly.

Sunshine, Clouds, and Shadows

The next morning, Erin found her mother and
Uncle Bub already up and chatting away in the sun
room when she got to the kitchen for her cereal.

"Here's to the mad scientist in the family," Uncle
Bub said, holding up his coffee cup in a mock toast.
Her mother lifted her cup, too, and added, "Hear,
hear!"

They were acting silly, Erin thought, but she
really didn't mind. It was going to be a great Science
Fair project, this strange seed from the faraway rain
forest. She took her cereal out to join them in the sun
room.

Uncle Bub leaned forward, slurping his coffee.
"How are you going to plan your science project?"
he asked.

"It will be a Before-and-After kind of display," Erin
answered quickly, for she had lain awake a long time
that night, excited about the prospects and thinking
about how she would go about organizing her project.
"First, I plan to show on a world map where the seed
probably came from and a description of it. Then I
want to display it growing exactly the way it would
look in the rain forest where it came from. It will be sort
of like solving a mystery, and nobody knows the
answer until we see the plant actually alive and
growing."

"Sounds great, Kiddo," her mother said. Then, to
Erin's amazement, her mother reached over and
poured the last few drops of coffee from her cup into

the big pot where Horace was growing, still limp and sickly-looking.

"Mom! What are you doing?" she exclaimed. "That's Horace—he's already sick, and now you're making him worse!"

"Horace? *That's* Horace?" her mother asked, astounded. "I thought that was the pineapple plant—Pinnochio or Pancreas or whatever its name is. You said I could always pour what little leftover coffee I might have in my cup on the pineapple plant because it would like it."

Erin slouched her shoulders and rolled her eyes. Uncle Bub laughed.

"Mom, *there's* the pineapple plant," Erin said, pointing to a tall spiked trunk nearby that didn't look at all like Horace. "That's Pericles. And coffee won't hurt him. But Horace is a Diffenbachia. How long have you been pouring leftover coffee on him?"

"Oh, well—for quite awhile, I'm afraid," she said, frowning. "I'm sorry—I just keep getting these plants mixed up. Do you think you may be able to save Horace?"

"Now that I know what the trouble is, yes," Erin said, with some relief. Poor Horace! All this time he had simply been drinking too much coffee!

Uncle Bub laughed and laughed.

When Erin got to school, she told Miss Barbary about her plans for her new Science Fair project. And she was surprised at how excited her teacher became.

"Excellent! Excellent!" Miss Barbary said. "Now, *that's* my idea of a good project. You must study the area of the world where the seed was found and duplicate the conditions exactly. The temperature, the humidity, amount of rainfall, sunlight—everything about it so that you can make it grow here. Your project should identify the family, the genus, and the species of the plant—to show how it fits into the known scientific world. Who knows? It may be just another household plant, like a Diffenbachia or a bromeliad,'' she added. ``After all, most of our common house plants come from the tropics. Or, better yet, it might turn out to be a fern, or one of those beautiful orchids that grow there. At any rate, displaying your research to identify and grow the plant will be an excellent project. Can you identify it by the seed?''

Erin wasn't prepared for so much interest in the project from her teacher.

"Well . . . no. No, I can't. Not yet, anyway," she stammered.

"Good! That means you'll be starting from scratch—an excellent project!" Miss Barbary said again. "Could be anything. That's the exciting part."

She jotted down some notes in her notebook.

"Probably the place to start would be to interview your uncle," she said, still writing. "Find out as much as you can about where he found the seed, what time of year it was, the kind of soil, the environment. . . . Get as many facts as you can, and then start from there with your research."

When she mentioned the slides that her uncle had taken of the rain forest and the washed-out area where the seed may have come from, Erin was again surprised at how excited Miss Barbary became.

"Wonderful!" she said, clasping her hands. "What a perfect way to round out our study unit on the environment! Do you think you could get your uncle to show us the slides in class tomorrow?"

Uncle Bub was delighted when Erin told him of Miss Barbary's request. While she was exchanging the old coffee-flavored soil for a new potting mixture for Horace that evening, Erin could hear him in the living room, sorting out his slides and practicing his remarks to go along with his slides. She could tell he was excited.

"You two children hurry up or you'll be late for school," Erin's mom said the next morning. She was taking great pleasure in the fact that Uncle Bub was also going to the sixth grade—back where he belonged, she said, laughing.

"You just leave Horace alone while we're away!" he yelled back as the kitchen door slammed behind them on their way to school. Horace had already started showing signs of recovery, thanks to the new potting soil.

"Miss Barbary, this is my Uncle . . . David," Erin said, when they arrived at school. Uncle Bub beamed at the use of his *real* name, and Erin felt somehow a little more grown up using it. Miss Barbary and Uncle Bub, Erin noticed, seemed to be getting along just fine. They chattered away about his trip to Belize as they set up the projector and screen. The students began drifting in, waiting for the bell to ring. Several congregated around Erin to learn more about what was in store for them once word had leaked out that it was her uncle who would be showing slides of the rain forest today. Among them, Erin was pleased to see, was Will Moreland, who seemed as excited as the others about today's special report.

Mrs. Oglethorp was there, too, waiting and watching quietly from the side of the room. She and Mr. Oglethorp had once taken a trip to Mexico to see the Mayan ruins, she told some nearby students, and she was interested in seeing scenes of neighboring Belize. "I'm sure there will be some similarities because the countries are so close," she explained. "And there could be some Mayan ruins there, too, as a consequence of natural migration." As usual, a number of the students looked at each other and stifled giggles when they heard her use the word *consequence.*

Soon Miss Barbary introduced their special guest for the day, and everybody settled back for Uncle Bub's presentation. But not for long. Will Moreland's hand shot up almost immediately, starting with the first photos of the rain forest taken from the airplane.

"How did you land?" he asked, watching scene after scene of thick rain forest stretching out for miles in every direction below the plane.

"A very good question," Uncle Bub said. "Keep in mind that the trees in the rain forest average around a hundred feet high. . . ."

Miss Barbary stepped forward and interrupted. "See that water tower out the window, class?" she asked, pointing to a tall, silvery tower a few blocks away. "It's about a hundred feet high, so that gives you some idea."

"Wow!" Will exclaimed, impressed.

"And some, which are called emergent trees, grow even higher than that," Uncle Bub said. Several *ooh's* emerged at random from around the classroom, and Erin felt good that his report was going so well.

"So here's where we landed," he added, and he clicked the projector to the next slide.

There was a gasp from the class. The picture showed the usual stretches of the rain forest from the air, but with what looked like a small hole cut out of the treetops.

"Are you kidding? How could you land in a space so small?" Will asked.

"Yeah," Ralph Sims added.

Uncle Bub laughed.

"It's misleading," he explained. "Actually, there was plenty of space to land once we got below the treetop level. Remember, you've still got a hundred feet to go before you land, and there's plenty of room down below for a small plane to land. But things grow so quickly in the rain forest that any open space fills with plants if the sun reaches the forest floor. So, they keep only this one small opening in the treetops for a plane to slip through during landing and takeoff. It's like flying into and out of a tunnel.''

"Are you a pilot?'' Nancy Bazemore asked.

"Not on this flight,'' Uncle Bub said, "but I'm a crew member on international flights for an airline, and they require that I have a pilot's license. And here,'' he said, moving to the next slide, "is one of the ugliest sights I've seen in all the world.''

There were many ooh's from the class at the scene of devastation on the screen. It was a picture of a vast wasteland, where all the vegetation had been cut down and burned away, leaving a scarred landscape of huge bald stumps, fragments of limbs and brush that jutted from the bare ground, and the remainders of burned piles of tree trunks and other vegetation. In the far distance, like a thin green line of life on an otherwise lifeless landscape, was the edge of the rain forest, and three big columns of smoke billowed from afar against the horizon.

"Oh, the consequences, the consequences,'' Mrs. Oglethorp said quietly, almost to herself, from the side of the room where she was standing with her arms folded, and for once the students didn't snicker when they heard her say the word consequences.

"That was the ugliest part of my trip to the rain forest,'' Uncle Bub said, "and this was one of the most interesting.'' He clicked to the next slide. It showed stone ruins of what once must have been a large building of some kind, with vague indentations carved in the massive pillars that still stood like the entrance to another place, another time. Except for the tall pillars, the ruins were almost covered with vines and other vegetation growing on the forest floor.

"I wish I could tell you the story of these ruins," Uncle Bub said. "But to tell the truth, they're so much like the rest of the rain forest in Belize: still 'undiscovered' in the official sense."

"What you have just heard is very true, class," Miss Barbary said. "Just yesterday, I was at a science conference at the university and was told that for every plant discovered in the rain forest, there are twenty that haven't yet been discovered."

"I thought just about everything on this planet had already been discovered," Will said, twisting in his seat and sounding a bit disappointed in the human race. He scoonched down in his desk, arms folded.

The slide show and Uncle Bub's narration proved to be a big hit with the sixth graders. They peppered him with questions until it was time for recess. The bell rang, and everybody filed out, still chattering about the rain forest and the slides.

"That does it," Mrs. Oglethorp said on her way out as she stopped to express her thanks for the slide show. "Frank is taking me to Belize this very summer."

"But those ruins may be gone by then," Miss Barbary said.

"They dare not be," the librarian said in all the authority she could muster, and left.

Erin lingered behind. She felt proud of Uncle Bub.

"They had very good questions," Uncle Bub said as he began packing away his slides. "You must be a good teacher, Miss Barbary."

"You're a good teacher yourself," Miss Barbary added. "I don't think I've ever seen the class so involved in a presentation. Erin is lucky to have an uncle like you.''

Erin blushed. *Let me get out of here,* she thought, and headed for the open door, where she was soon surrounded by her friends, still excited about the presentation.

When she got home that afternoon after school, Uncle Bub was waiting to ask Erin about the reactions to his report. She assured him it had been a huge success. *What were some of the comments like?* he wanted to know, so she told him many of the exact comments and who made them. He was clearly pleased; but regardless of how many good things she reported to him, he still seemed to be fishing for more, for something else.

''But what about Miss Barbary? What did she say?'' he finally asked.

Aha! Erin thought, understanding now that Uncle Bub might be attracted to Miss Barbary. A smile crossed her face, and she began sauntering away, holding her head in the air.

''Oh,'' she said lazily, nonchalantly, ''nothing that you'd be interested in hearing, I'm sure.''

''The Niece from the House of Horror!'' Uncle Bub yelled, laughing, and threw a cushion at her.

Later, as they ate dinner, Erin explained that Miss Barbary asked her to bring the seed to class so that she might provide some clue about its genus or species to help Erin get started.

''And in the meantime,'' she added, ''she told me that I should interview you, Uncle Bub—to get all the facts I could on exactly where you found the seed, the time of year, the temperature, the kinds of plants.''

"But I didn't find the seed; it found me!" Uncle Bub protested. "As for the time of year, it was just a few days ago, the temperature was hot, it was raining, and there weren't any other plants around because the rain forest had all been cut down. I'm afraid I'm not going to be much help, Kiddo, but I'll try."

So after dinner, Uncle Bub and Erin sprawled out on the living room floor with maps and brochures and books about Belize and the rain forests there.

"When you plant the seed, Erin," Uncle Bub said, "if you want to duplicate the conditions in the rain forest, maybe the soil should have a lot of dead leaves and decaying matter because that's what covered the forest floor."

"Compost," Erin's mother said, looking up from the magazine she was reading. "Even I know that!"

"Very good, Mom," Erin said. "And you're right. What else can you tell me, Uncle Bub?"

"Well, be sure it gets lots of water, because it rains there every day. Does it ever! You have my word on that!"

On a map, he traced his trip from the coast to the interior of the rain forest but added that he might be miles and miles off target because he was never able to tell which direction the rickety bus had taken.

"But you're a navigator," Erin's mother interrupted. "You should know these technical things. Humph!"

"The little plane I flew in went due west," he said, "but down on the rain forest floor, with only occasional shafts of sunlight filtering through, it was almost impossible to keep a sense of direction about where the bus was heading. It just seemed to take the path of least resistance. Besides, I was too busy looking to figure out exactly which direction we were going. So there—put that in your coffee mug and give it to Horace!''

''Humph,'' Erin's mother said again, and went back to reading her magazine.

Erin wished that she had been able to get more precise information from Uncle Bub to help plan her Science Fair project. Although it didn't seem like much, he had given her enough for a start. And tomorrow, Miss Barbary would study the seed and give her some idea about its genus and species.

''Thanks, Uncle Bub,'' she said, gathering her materials from the floor. ''You've given me a good start.''

''Good luck on your project,'' he said, standing and stretching and yawning. ''I have to leave tomorrow, but I'll be back in a few weeks to check on how it's going. I expect to see this place turned into one big tropical bloom when I come back.''

Erin always hated to see him go, but she knew that he'd be back again soon. The next morning, she hugged him goodbye, and he made her promise to tell Miss Barbary how much he enjoyed his visit to her classroom. She left for school feeling lonely, but the feeling was mixed with excitement as her hand closed around the carefully-wrapped seed in her pocket.

After school, Miss Barbary carefully unwrapped the seed and examined it, turning it over and into different positions with a pair of tweezers.

''Humm,'' she murmured from time to time, and jotted down notes. Twice she opened a huge book titled *Taxonomic Keys* and turned to various pages. But the more she studied, the deeper her frown became.

''Well,'' she finally said, quietly closing the book,

``this one certainly is not giving up any clues about its ancestry. Every path I've tried to follow has led to a dead end. Now I'm really intrigued, Erin,'' she said, and Erin felt that she was talking to her almost as a colleague rather than as a teacher to a student. ``Tell me, did the little village have a name where your uncle found the seed?''

``It wasn't in a village,'' Erin answered, trying to sound as grown up as she could, the way she felt a real scientist would. ``It was out in a huge open area where the rain forest had been cut away.''

Miss Barbary shook her head. ``Double trouble,'' she said. ``Do you know if your uncle plans to go back there anytime soon?''

``He never knows,'' Erin answered. ``The airline sends him everywhere, and it changes from one month to the next. I could ask him the next time he calls.''

``No, never mind. It really wouldn't help, because we couldn't duplicate the conditions again exactly as they happened. Besides, from what he told me, I don't think your Uncle David would care to get back on that rickety bus again during the monsoon season.''

They laughed together, and Miss Barbary walked Erin to the classroom door.

``We'll just work with what we have,'' she said. ``Tell you what: let me keep this seed until tomorrow, and we'll take it over to Professor Briscoe at the university. I'm sure he can give us a really good analysis of its species—or at least its genus. I've drawn a complete blank trying to figure out either one. Ask your mother if you can go along; I'll drop you off at your house if she agrees.''

On the way home, the little black cloud that had been named Horace no longer floated above Erin's head, because she knew Horace was home and already showing sure signs of recovery. And, now with Miss Barbary's help, the Science Fair project was no longer a little black cloud—if anything, it had turned into something shiny and promising.

If only, if only, if only, she thought. If only the rain forest seed turned out to be something spectacular that would overshadow Will Moreland's entire solar system.

Bloom Where You Are Planted

"Let's see what we have here," Professor Briscoe said, leaning back heavily in his squeaking office chair and carefully unfolding the napkin from around the seed which Erin had given him. He was a big, tall man with a shock of white hair and a kindly face. His collar didn't quite come together close enough to button, and his tie was off-center and draped to one side. He adjusted his little round glasses and peered at the seed.

"Well, well, well," he said mostly to himself. And then again, "Well, well, well." Miss Barbary and Erin looked at each other and made a *well, what?* face.

"I exhausted all of my references, Dr. Briscoe," Miss Barbary said. "So I was hoping you might help us identify what kind of plant we can expect for Erin's Science Fair project."

"I can tell you this," he said, gently turning the seed in his fingers. "It should not be left without moisture for much longer. See these tiny green tendrils that encase it? I notice that they're already beginning to dry out on the ends. If this comes from the rain forest as you say, it may already have been without moisture too long to germinate."

Erin's heart did a flip-flop.

"But for the most part, it seems to be in fairly good shape. Certainly it is worth a try. You have come up with a good project, young lady," he said to Erin. "Who knows what we have here? Rain forests have been around for 100 million years. Nowadays they're a magnet for botanists and zoologists from all over the world, who visit them to discover all the secrets they can before it's too late. But there's still so much to be done. Rain forests are home to half the earth's plant and animal species, although they occupy only two percent of the earth's surface.''

"And now even less than that," Miss Barbary said. "They're being destroyed at such a terrible rate."

Professor Briscoe shook his head sadly. "Yes, I know. It is tragic. What people don't seem to realize is that the less rain forest, the less rain. Those millions of acres they've cut down can't be watered like a vegetable garden to make things grow again. What's done is done.

"Let's go to the lab," he said, and they followed him across the hall. He unlocked the door and flicked on the light, and Erin's eyes grew wide. Plants of all sizes, shapes, and descriptions lined the tables and shelves in the huge room. They were in what looked like glass tanks of some kind. The air had a peculiar, pungent odor to it, something like the potting soil she used for her plants at home, except stronger. There were tanks with bubbling water, tanks filled with colored rocks of some kind, tanks with what looked like little blobs of gelatin, tanks filled with plastic particles of different colors, and tanks filled with dry sand. And growing in the tanks were the plants—some looking glossy and healthy and luxuriant, others looking malnourished and sickly—worse than Horace ever did.

"Science is nothing spectacular," the professor said when he saw Erin looking at the plants. "Colorless but careful." He walked over to one of the tables and motioned Erin to come near. "Do you recognize what plant this is?" he asked.

Erin studied the plant. A big spray of leaf-covered limbs grew out of a slim, short trunk that barely emerged from the soil where it was growing. The limbs were long and slender, with soft-looking leaves that seemed to cling shyly to the stem where they grew. It could have been some sort of little tree, or maybe a big bush. She wasn't sure.

"Have you ever been to Texas?" the professor asked. "Out in the western part of the state?"

No, Erin told him, although her Uncle Bub had lived there once.

"This is a tumbleweed," Professor Briscoe said, smiling. "They grow wild there. Let me tell you about it and why we have this one here. What you are looking at is a masterpiece of survival and conquest. First, the tumbleweed grows in the prairie where the land is flat with little vegetation and the winds blows a lot. So what does it do? Well, most plants are content to grow wherever they find themselves and go through the usual cycles of blooming, bearing fruit, and propagating. But not this fellow. Oh,

no. Somehow and in some way, it sensed that the land was flat and the wind blew a lot. So its limbs, just like these you see here, started to grow back to toward the center to make the whole thing in the rough shape of a ball. Then it grew a very thin, weak

trunk so that the whole ball of limbs would snap off in a breeze, and away the whole thing would go!— tumbling across the prairie, and of course every time it hit a bump, its seeds scattered in every direction. It's almost like a well-designed, self-perpetuating machine. Brilliant, I tell you! Brilliant! While the other plants stayed in one spot, this one took off for the wide blue yonder! So we brought this one here to see how many generations it would need before it sensed that there's no prairie nearby and its old tricks won't work around here. I wonder how long it will take, don't you? Ten generations? Ten years? A million years? Who knows?''

He wheeled around and headed to the far end of the laboratory and flicked several switches on a stack of machines that took up most of the wall space at that end. A panel of lights and gauges lit up.

''He was my favorite professor when I was in college,'' Miss Barbary said quietly to Erin as they followed him to the far end of the lab. ''He made me love science. He loves to study plants. Maybe one day you'll study under him when you get to college— especially since you're the future botanist in our class.''

Erin was taken aback at the idea of college. *But I'm just in the sixth grade,* she thought. *What do I know about college? I've still got to pass all those courses in high school.*

Still, she found the idea exciting as she gazed at the long rows of plant experiments in the lab. Then a thought occurred to her, a thought she might hesitate to tell any other living soul, even her mother, but it seemed okay to share it with Miss Barbary.

''Sometimes I think I'd like to spend the whole day every day just working with plants,'' she confided to Miss Barbary—"making sure they're healthy, and changing the soil mixture to suit their needs, or changing the temperature or amount of water to make them grow better, trying different ways of planting seeds and getting them to germinate. . . ."

Miss Barbary laughed. "Then you want to be exactly like Professor Briscoe," she said. "Because that's what he does, and he loves it. And he makes others like me love it, too. That's what professors do. Maybe you ought to think about becoming a professor of botany."

Erin was dumbfounded. "Is that what professors do?" she asked. "Just spend their whole time studying whatever they're interested in?"

"Basically, yes," Miss Barbary said, smiling. "And when they study enough and teach others about what they're doing, they become experts, specialists. Like Professor Briscoe, for instance. Let's see what he's up to."

Professor Briscoe had placed the rain forest seed on a small metal platform under a piece of glass.

"We know what the outside looks like," he said, "but unfortunately that doesn't help us much with identification as I had hoped. So we'll use this spectroscope to see if there's anything we can find out about the property of those unusual colors on its surface. I'd like to know how deep they go and what function they serve. Very unusual."

He pressed a button on the bank of machines, and a metal plate came down to conceal the seed from view. Then a series of flashing lights followed.

"This will give us the equivalent of an x-ray," the professor said, "but without the dangers. I would imagine that an infra-red invasion would be disastrous for such a seed as this. We have to be very careful in using even the slightest amount of radiation when working with raw seeds," he continued. "I've seen entire experiments wiped out."

Something clicked on the machine, and the metal plate withdrew. Erin was glad to see the seed looked the same.

"Seeds are among the most sensitive things in nature," Professor Briscoe continued. "One drop of moisture at the right time on an acorn will produce a hundred-foot oak tree a century later. But the timing is important. You must treat this seed very carefully. It's out of its element."

"We'll have to get it into the right culture as soon as possible," Miss Barbary said to Erin.

"Tell me, young lady," the professor said to Erin. "Do you know what the term *symbiosis* means?"

Erin felt a stab of fear. More than anything she wanted to say *yes.* But she had no earthly idea.

"Oh, no—not yet," Miss Barbary broke in. "That's a concept that isn't taught until high school. Unless, of course, Erin happens to know it on her own. Do you, Erin?"

Erin blushed and said, "I'm afraid not," grateful that Miss Barbary had rescued her.

"Well, it's an interesting idea, especially where the rain forest is concerned. You see, once one kind of plant or animal dies in the rain forest, others that depend on it die, too. Every living thing there depends in some way on another living thing." He opened a drawer and took out a thick pad of white paper and, to Erin's surprise, began sketching a picture of the seed.

"Right here in our town, for instance," he continued, "suppose something happened to the honeybees. The flower population, especially the flowering shrubs, would be greatly diminished for lack of pollination. And in the rain forests, the balance is even more fragile."

He continued sketching a picture of the seed as he talked, drawing arrows to different parts and jotting notes in the margin, and Erin could see that it was a very detailed drawing and very good.

"Survival of the rain forest depends on the interrelationships of the plants and animals that live there. And many times it defies all logic. You can't explain what works there and why. For example, one of the world's slowest animals, the three-toed sloth, is also one of the most successful in the rain forest. And here in this country, one of our most endangered plants is a tiny white bell-shaped flower called the Oconee Bell. It grows in only two places in the world: a small area of South Carolina where the winters are short and mild, and in another small area in the state of Maine, where the winters are long and harsh. Who can explain it?"

He thumped the pad of paper with his pencil and placed them back in the drawer. "That will suffice until I can study the results further," he said. Then he leaned back in his chair, crossed his arms, and looked across at Miss Barbary.

"And I suppose, Miss Barbary," he said, "that you have already told our young botanist here about my pet theory?"

Miss Barbary laughed. "Oh, no, Dr. Briscoe. I'll let you tell her about that."

"I have long held this theory," he said to Erin,

``that plants are an alternate form of life from outer space.''

Erin looked at Miss Barbary, who was smiling at the professor.

``Think about it,'' he said. ``Members of the animal kingdom, like people or birds or insects, are free to move around, to find food or water, to go where we want. So we spend our lives running around doing whatever it is we feel we need to do before we die. But plants, on the other hand, can't do that. Where they are born, they stay, and they spend their entire life right there, where they've got food and light and water—whatever it takes to keep them going. I think plants are pretty smart forms of life—probably a lot more intelligent than animals, if we could communicate with them. *Bloom where you are*

planted. That's what plants are telling us. *Stop all this running around and messing things up. Bloom where you are planted.''*

The professor looked again at Miss Barbary, and this time he chuckled. It was a quiet kind of chuckle from deep down that made his shoulders shake. And Erin was relieved to hear Miss Barbary laugh with him.

''Erin, don't be alarmed,'' she said. ''Dr. Briscoe gives that speech to all his beginning students— except in more detail,'' she added, laughing again. ''It's his way to get them to look at plants in a new way, as something different and exciting.''

''And who knows?'' the professor said, clicking off the switches and starting down the lab toward the door. ''I've never really told them whether I believe my theory or not. It keeps them wondering. What do you think, Erin?''

Erin surprised herself at how quickly she answered. ''Oh, no. I don't think plants are from outer space,'' she said. ''They belong right here on earth.'' Then a thought occurred to her, and she tried to stifle a giggle as she thought about Will Moreland. ''People might come from outer space, but not plants.'' The three of them laughed and laughed as they left the lab and Professor Briscoe switched off the overhead lights and locked the door.

''The seed you have brought is most peculiar,'' he said as they walked across the hall to his office. ''My first inclination was to classify it under *Bromelia,* which is a very large genus of grasses that includes such plants as pineapples and bromeliads, for example. But there's also a hint of the *Digitalis* genus in its formation, too. To be honest, I simply must withhold judgment for now until I can do some further investigation or until I see the plant itself.''

He wrapped the seed on a little cotton pad, placed it in a white box, and handed it to Erin.

''My suggestion is that you lose no time in getting this planted,'' he said. ''In the rain forests, plants have no winter. They can grow, bloom, and bear fruit at any time of the year. The right combination. All they need is the right combination, just like the drop of water on the acorn at just the right time.''

Erin took the seed. It now seemed like such a breakable, fragile thing in her hand. She was almost afraid to move it, for fear that she might disturb some delicate mechanism inside. How different it seemed now from the first time she saw it, when she and her mom and Uncle Bub had pitched it to each other like some kind of silly souvenir.

''Thank you, Professor Briscoe,'' Miss Barbary said. ''We appreciate your help, and we'll get started on this project right away. I hope you plan to attend the Science Fair.''

''Haven't missed it in years,'' he answered. ''You may be sure I'll be there. And I will let you know what I find out about the seed as soon as I can check a few more references. Good luck on your project, young lady. I look forward to seeing how it turns out.''

''Thank you,'' Erin said shyly. She felt so tiny next to this big, towering man. But she liked him. She hoped she would see him again. And she felt she would.

After Miss Barbary dropped her off at home, Erin went straight to the sun room. She gingerly placed the box with the seed on the shelf next to Pericles the

Pineapple. *Who knows?* she thought. *The two of you may be distant cousins. Or even close kin.*

She began searching for just the right pot in which to plant the seed. It had to be the right size and shape so she could move it around the room, either into or out of the sun as needed, or near a window or away from a vent—whatever the plant might seem to need as it was growing.

It had to grow. It just had to!

The temperature, the humidity, the amount of moisture in the soil, even the soil itself—everything had to be ``the right combination,'' in Professor Briscoe's words. That's what she had to find. She had already listed the average temperature of Belize and the amount of rainfall per year. And compost, her all-knowing mom's compost, for soil, like Uncle Bub described. As she began gathering the materials, her thoughts flew ahead to the day of the Science Fair. She could picture her booth. There, forming a backdrop would be a huge atlas of the world, with an arrow pointing to Belize. Then, stand-up charts would display her research: average temperature, average rainfall, major rivers, population, size, acres of rain forest land before and after the cutting and burning. . . . Suddenly remembering the desolate scenes of the vast burned-out wasteland in Uncle Bub's slides, she felt a strange and deep sympathy for the seed. *What green, glorious place did you come from?* she wondered, looking at the little box where the seed lay protected like some kind of jewel. *And what is it like now? Is it still there? Do you have a home to go back to, even if you could?* She remembered the professor's silly theory about the difference in plants and animals, except now it didn't seem quite so silly after all.

When everything was ready, she gently took the seed out of the box and placed it on a stool next to Claire and Pericles, with Horace and Priscilla and Clementine in the background. Then she went into the storage closet in the hallway and got her Mom's camera.

``Don't stay up too late now, Kiddo,'' her mom said from her bedroom, where she lay in bed reading.

``I won't, Mom. Just a little longer. Got to get this seed in the soil. It won't be long. Good night.''

``Spring planting, huh?'' her mom said, and Erin could tell she was on the edge of sleep. ``Good Night, Kiddo.''

Erin took close-up photos of the seed from as many angles as she could, and hoped that some would be sharp and clear and colorful enough to display as part of her project. As she continued to take photos, she remembered the professor's remark about infra-red rays and how sensitive seeds are.

I can't wait any longer, she said to herself. With more care than she ever remembered taking before, she planted the seed. As she gently covered it with the damp potting soil that she had prepared and then patted it into place, she wondered if it could sense the earth around it again, if it could feel that it was home once more, free to begin its magic cycle of growing and reaching through the earth and into the air, filling its space with leaves and flowers.

Have I planted you the right way? she found

herself asking. *Is this close enough to the right combination?*

The right combination. She was determined to find it, whatever it was. *Please, please,* she said to herself and to the plant. *Bloom where you are planted.*

The Seed of Destruction

First she thought the amount of sun might not be quite right, so she moved it to a spot between Clementine and Thomas, where there was a dappling of shade and sun during most of the day. Then the temperature in the room seemed a bit cool, so she turned up the thermostat a couple of degrees. After all, this was a tropical rain forest she was trying to emulate, and the equator was a land without winters, as Professor Briscoe had said. Next, she added a little more water each day, because Uncle Bub said it had rained there every afternoon, and heavy rain at that. Then, remembering again how bright and blinding the sun seemed in the photos of the desolate landscape where the forest had been cleared away, she finally decided to put the pot in the window, where it would be first to feel the warm sun each day.

It was driving Erin crazy, this strange seed from a strange world. She worried about it every day. It was the first thing she thought about each morning, and it was the last thing she thought about each night. Was it getting too much sun now? Or not enough? Maybe a little more water every day. Or would that be too much? And how low does the temperature get at night in Belize? Maybe the thermostat should be turned down each night and back up the next morning. She moved the pot with the seed in it around almost every day, changing her mind, trying something different—a few degrees difference in the temperature, a little more sun, a little less water, then a little less sun, a little more water. . . .

"Just like me when you were a child, Kiddo," her mother said. "Sometimes, you just have to do your best and hope everything turns out okay. When you were still just a baby, I read all kinds of books about how to bring up an infant properly and took all kinds of advice from just about everybody—and almost went crazy in the process, just like you're doing now. So, after awhile, I just decided to go with my instincts, do the best that I could, and let the chips fall where they may. And you know what? It worked! Now I've got a daughter just like me, perfect in every way!" She poured herself another cup of coffee. "So it works. Just do your best, Kiddo, and don't worry about it."

Erin sat at the kitchen table with her chin resting on the palm of one hand.

"I know, Mom," she said, without moving. "But I

just can't help worrying about it. My whole Science Fair project depends on growing this seed, and there's not one sign of life after all this time. It just lies there, silent under the soil. I've tried everything, and there's still nothing happening.''

''Maybe it's just sleeping awhile,'' her mother said. ''After all, remember that it made a long trip to get here, several thousand miles, and has been through a lot. Maybe it's just tired. Maybe it's under there right this minute, blinking its little eyes, stretching, and trying to wake up.''

Erin didn't think so. She smiled at her mother's image of the seed as a little baby, but she felt there was good reason to worry. From everything that she could determine, almost every kind of growth in the rain forest is rapid, and the seed should have shown some signs of life by now. Even regular flower seeds which she remembered planting years before had always sprouted in a matter of days.

She walked into the sun room and looked at the pot again. Still nothing. It sat there in its latest resting place, on the wide windowsill between Horace and Claire now, with no sign of life. Then a slight shudder went through Erin. Could she be looking at a tiny grave? She quickly dismissed the idea and walked over to the window. Outside there were new forms of life popping up everywhere to herald a new spring. It was a mint morning, cool and green and clean in a pastel world, with a pale blue sky to match and a few bright fluffs of white clouds dappled here and there. The shrubbery was covered in bright new leaves for the season, standing in glossy contrast to last year's old growth. Splashes of color decorated the landscape with patches of crocus and daffodils, and a few wandering wisps of wisteria draped their grape-like clusters of blossoms from an occasional high limb in the trees. A carpet of fresh green grass provided the backdrop for the whole picture, and Erin could almost feel the urging and energy of new springtime life budding forth everywhere. She turned to the lifeless pot.

Come on, come on, she thought. *Don't you see all this? Can't you sense what's going on all around you? Why don't you do something?*

She walked over and impulsively brushed a few particles of soil off the top. There was nothing there, and she quickly replaced it, patting it tenderly in place. Maybe she had planted the seed too deep in the soil. Maybe it should be nearer the surface. If she dug it up this very minute and checked to see if it showed any signs of germination, then she could plant it right back where it was and still have time to make it to school. But then she remembered Professor Briscoe's words: *seeds are among the most sensitive things in nature.* Even if she found the seed showing signs of germinating, it might go into shock if it were moved now.

She shook her head. She didn't know what to do. So she wheeled around, grabbed her books, pecked her mom on the cheek, and headed for the door.

Her mom looked up from the morning paper. ``Any sign?'' she asked, and Erin knew that, although her mom still didn't know anything about plants, she did care about this project because it was important to Erin.

``So far, nothing,'' Erin called back. `` 'Bye, Mom,'' as the door slammed behind her.

At school, by the end of the day, Miss Barbary had experienced nothing but trouble in competing for the students' attention against the pull of the beautiful spring day waiting outside for them. As they entered the last period, her exasperation had turned into a slow burn. Erin could tell that the entire class was in for one humongous Silent Scold.

It had started out fairly well.

``Class, today I want to go down the rows and have each of you give us a progress report on your Science Fair project,'' Miss Barbary had said. ``Remember, it's only a few short weeks, so you should be far enough along in your plans to tell us how your project is going. Now is a good time to compare notes. By sharing what you are doing with others, we can avoid having our projects all look alike. So pay attention to what each person has to say, and feel free to ask each other questions or make suggestions as we go along.''

She started with Will, who of course was sitting in his front-row seat, eager to be first.

``My project is going *great!*'' he said. ``At first I had planned just to show the solar system, which I'm still going to do, but now I intend to add movement, too, to show how they revolve in the universe. Can you imagine that? The planets will actually turn. It's going to show the sun, too, and why we have night and day because whatever side of a planet the sun doesn't hit—that's night. And—oh, yeah—the moons, too! Except there's a slight problem with Pluto, because it's so far away from the other planets that I can't figure out how to connect it to the others without throwing everything off balance. . . .''

"I think we get the idea, Will, thank you," Miss Barbary said.

"But I think I've figured out how to solve the problem," he added quickly. "Mr. Oglethorp is going to help me. Is that all right if we get grownups to help us, Miss Barbary?"

"Certainly," she said. "The whole idea behind the Science Fair is to help you students learn about the world through the scientific method of investigation. As long as it's your idea for your project, you can certainly get help from others in setting it up and arranging the project. So long as it's your project and you are the one doing all the learning."

"Great!" said Will, again rising to his favorite position of standing on his knees in his desk. "Because it *is* my idea, and I know it'll work. Mr. Oglethorp said he'd help. It's going to be magNIFicent!"

Oh, that word, Erin thought to herself from the other side of the room. *If it's not Will Moreland, it's Uncle Bub using that silly word.* Her thoughts drifted to Uncle Bub. She wondered where he was right this minute—probably in some faraway place in the world, maybe even finding her another interesting souvenir. Then she thought of the seed. It wasn't really a souvenir. It had just happened, had just appeared in her life, without anybody planning on it. Now she almost wished it hadn't. Her spirits sagged. Sooner or later, Miss Barbary would call on her, and she would have to admit that her project was turning out to be a dud—a real dud. Maybe that's what she ought to name the seed: *Dud.*

But then that thought made her feel guilty. It wasn't the seed's fault that it didn't grow. It was hers—her fault. She didn't do something right. She hadn't found what Professor Briscoe had called "the right combination." But she wasn't going to give up. Not yet. Especially not after hearing Will Moreland's big plans.

Miss Barbary continued down the rows, but it became clear very soon that many of the students had given very little thought to their science projects—and some not at all. The air in the classroom soon seemed to press down on the students like the weight of a heavy cloud carrying the threat of a communal SS—and even with the prospect of some thunder and lightning.

"It is clear to me that some of you have given little or no thought to these projects," she said, in an even kind of voice that sounded as if it had been measured by a yardstick. "For your information, the Science Fair is one of the most important things we will be doing this year, because your work will be displayed before the entire community. Everyone will be viewing it—not only your friends and all the other students in this school but also your parents and other adults, merchants and businesses, civic leaders—everybody. I will not tolerate second-rate projects, I will not tolerate third-rate ideas, and I will not tolerate fourth-rate thinking. I want nothing but a first-rate effort from you. All of you. First rate."

Then she picked up where she had left off.

"Ralph Sims, I believe you are next. According to my notes, your project is going to show the various stages that frogs go through in their development, from tadpoles to mature frogs. That sounds interesting. It's a good local biology project. How far along are you?" she asked.

Ralph squirmed in his seat.

``Can I change my topic?'' he finally asked meekly.

Miss Barbary's mouth tightened, and the students felt the SS cloud frost over as it hung above them in the room, now dripping icicles.

``It is too late to be changing projects in mid-stream,'' she said tightly. ``Why aren't you keeping your first choice?''

``I've looked everywhere, Miss Barbary, but there aren't any tadpoles to be found,'' Ralph said. ``But I remember seeing them last year in just about every little puddle—millions of them. Now I can't find a one, not a single one. Maybe the timing is off or something.''

Tell me about it, Erin thought. *Tell me about timing,* as she pictured the seed waiting motionless at home.

Surprisingly, Ralph's comment about timing seemed to hit a responsive chord with Miss Barbary.

``Yes, you are right about that, Ralph,'' she said. ``Timing is important, and it's a good lesson for all of you to learn. Class, when it comes to Mother Nature, you must remember that nothing is automatic. The forces of nature are very unpredictable, because the balance of nature is so fragile and can be upset so easily. This year, for instance, there may be some kind of virus or disease that could have decimated the local frog population. It could be anything. You never know. Or it could be that the weather has delayed the usual cycle, and it may be weeks from now before the eggs are hatched. At any rate, Ralph, what alternate project have you chosen?''

``The pomato plants—or topato, or whatever they're called,'' he said, desperately hoping to evoke more laughter as he did before and break the ice from the cloud hanging above. But he obviously failed. The class by now was too nervous to laugh, considering Miss Barbary's impatience with them and their projects. Ralph turned to look at Erin. "You know, the plants with tomatoes on top and potatoes on the bottom—the ones that Erin talked about at first. Before she changed her mind."

"Very well," Miss Barbary said, and jotted the new choice next to Ralph's name in her notebook. "But remember, Ralph: you have only a few short weeks before the Science Fair, so you may not have enough time to grow adult plants. Be sure to illustrate what you are doing and what the final results will look like."

I can't even do that, Erin thought. *I don't have any idea what the final result might look like. If it even grows. Which it probably won't.*

"And yes, Erin has chosen a different project," Miss Barbary said. "A very interesting one—an unknown seed from the rain forest."

"It sounds weird," Nancy Bazemore said. "It might even be poison or something."

"Yes. Well, Erin's project is to study the seed and identify it from what little evidence she has," Miss Barbary said, obviously still pleased with Erin's choice. "It's a good example of using scientific principles to learn about the world we live in. So that by the time the plant grows, we will know what it is and what it will look like, based on Erin's research."

"The seed of destruction," Will Moreland said in a low voice from across the room, but not too low for Erin to hear. Miss Barbary heard it, too, and turned to look at Will. Her scowl suggested that the scold was probably not going to be a silent one this time.

Brrinnnggg!

"Tomorrow! Tomorrow! We'll finish these first thing," Miss Barbary yelled over the sixth-grade eruption out of the classroom at the sound of the final bell. It was clear that they were eager to end the day, and probably Miss Barbary was, too.

This time, Erin realized, both she and Will were saved by the bell, but for different reasons.

She quickly stuffed her books into her booksack, slung it over her shoulders, and took the long way around the back of the room on her way out to avoid the possibility that Miss Barbary might ask for a progress report on her project anyway—especially when there wasn't any. She had planted the seed. That's all she could tell, and that wasn't much progress.

The seed of destruction. How silly, she thought as she walked home. *And how correct, probably.* Will Moreland was still a pest, but she knew he was smart, too, and his Science Fair project had the sound of a winner.

"Three guesses," her mother said when Erin got home.

Erin brightened a bit.

"Is it good news?" she asked, pitching her booksack into her room and plopping down on the living room sofa next to her mom. "I could use it."

"Only the best," her mom said.

"You got a raise?" Erin asked.

"Oh, my goodness, no—but that would be the best kind of news, I admit. You got a letter from your Uncle Bub," she said, pitching an envelope to Erin.

"Is he coming back here soon?" Erin asked, tearing at the big square envelope.

"I wouldn't know. He didn't write *me*," her mother said in a haughty voice, pretending to take offense at being slighted.

Erin smiled and opened the envelope. It was a big card, with a beautiful painting of an egret on the front, framed with the graceful green fronds of a fern. She opened it to find Uncle Bub's usual big scrawling penmanship inside.

"As usual, he writes big so he won't have to say much," her mother observed.

"He's going to be here in three weeks," Erin said, reading. "And this time he's going to be able to stay with us longer. Wonderful!"

"Where is he now?" her mother asked, trying to read over Erin's shoulder.

"In the Sahara desert—can you believe it?" Erin said, smiling.

"Maybe he'll bring you back a lizard or something." her mother said, taking the card from Erin to read it for herself. "Oh, what a beautiful card!"

Erin walked into the kitchen and opened the refrigerator door.

"I'm glad for some good news for a change," she called to her mother. "Uncle Bub's going to be here—oh, no! That means he'll probably be here during the Science Fair!" She closed the refrigerator door and poured a glass of milk. "I bet he's going to be really disappointed to see how our famous rain forest project turns out to be a dud at the Science Fair!''

''Nonsense,'' her mother said, ''Oh, by the way, I almost forgot. You'll be so proud of me. Take a look in the sun room.''

Now what? Erin asked herself, knowing that the prospect of her mother loose in the sun room was roughly equivalent to a dinosaur loose on main street. She glanced around and saw nothing different. Everything seemed in its place.

''What is it?'' she asked, sipping her milk. ''I don't see anything different.''

''Take a closer look,'' her mother said proudly. ''I discovered it myself. Aren't you proud of me?''

Erin's heart quickened. She plopped down her glass of milk and rushed over to the pot in the windowsill. There, sure enough, the soil had cracked just the slightest bit, and a tender-looking tendril, milky-white with just the slightest hint of green, was peeking from underneath.

It was growing. The seed was growing!

She vowed never to use the word *dud* again for as long as she lived.

Those Good Gommy Gloppies

Slowly but surely, and so very slowly that sometimes Erin thought it had stopped altogether, the plant grew. Each morning she rushed into the sun room first thing to check on it, and she even kept a tiny ruler handy to record how much, if any, it had grown since the day before. Its one leaf inched from the soil on a nondescript stem and turned into an agonizingly unremarkable something that looked like just about every other leaf in the world.

Along with the daily measurements she was taking, Erin also jotted down where the plant had been placed that day in the room, hoping to find that maybe it grew more rapidly in the sun than it did in the shade, or preferred some kind of combination. She tried different temperatures at night and during the day, different amounts of water, and dutifully recorded any changes. One day she even placed a radio nearby to see if the plant responded to music, but then she wasn't sure which kind of music to play and gave up on the idea.

Nothing seemed to matter. The plant just kept up its slow pace, like a three-toed sloth, of slowly enlarging its one leaf. And as days turned into weeks, Erin became frantic. The Science Fair was practically here; and in spite of all that she had done, she realized that she was going to have the world's most unspectacular plant to display for her project. The only hope, which happened just two days before the Science Fair, was a second leaf which appeared almost overnight. But it was only one-fourth the size of the first one—nothing more than a miniature copy and just as nondescript. And, just like the first one, it showed no signs of wanting to grow into anything but another boring leaf.

Then, whether Erin was ready or not, two things happened almost simultaneously the same day: Uncle Bub arrived, and the day of the Science Fair dawned. He had brought her a beautiful pair of cloth slippers, and the Science Fair had brought her a black cloud.

''Don't worry about the plant, Kiddo,'' Uncle Bub said. ''It's your research that's supposed to be the important part, and it's great. I've read it and have learned more about that plant and Belize and the rain forest than I ever dreamed possible—and I've been there!''

''Sure,'' her mom said. ''And remember what I told you: sometimes you just do the best you can

and let the chips fall where they may. It'll be fine. You'll see.''

Erin carefully packed up all of her charts and and the posters with the color photos of the seed on them and placed them in the back seat of her mom's car. *Maybe Uncle Bub is right,* she thought. *Maybe the judges will look at my research reports and all the data I've collected about the rain forest and won't care what the plant looks like. After all, they'll be looking for a science project, not a spectacular plant.* She felt a little better.

She went back inside to get the plant and take it out to the car. But when she saw it again, still sitting there in its same drab position, her hopes sank in spite of what Uncle Bub had said. She took it out and placed it on the floor of the car. *Maybe Mom is right, after all. You just do your best and don't worry about it,* she thought.

She went back inside to where they sat at the kitchen table. "I guess I'm ready," she said.

Her mother dropped Erin and Uncle Bub off near the end of the school building at the multi-purpose room.

"I'll be by early this afternoon as soon as they open the doors," she called. "Good luck!" And she inched her car away through the traffic jam of other parents bringing cars loaded with other projects. It was a madhouse, and Erin felt the excitement of it all. Her classmates were lugging in huge boxes of all kinds of materials, and there were parents trying to maneuver through the crowds with arms full of huge posters and charts and graphs.

"What on earth do you suppose that is?" Uncle Bub asked Erin as a man rushed past them holding a strange-looking apparatus made up of strings and pulleys and levers, all of which seemed to be falling apart.

"There's no telling," Erin said. "There are so many different projects." She carried the pot with the rain forest plant in it while Uncle Bub followed along, trying to balance the posters and charts she had prepared for her display. They squeezed through the crowd that congregated around the doorway and finally got inside. It was a huge room, with a big open area in the middle and tables lining the walls on two sides. The other students and their parents were busy dumping the materials on the tables, and some had already started setting up the displays.

Erin soon located the space allotted for her project on one of the tables; and as soon as she and Uncle Bub had put their materials down, a number of students crowded around. They remembered Uncle Bub from his slide presentation to the class earlier in the year.

"Our rain forest man," they called him, and a few looked at the plant sitting on the table but said nothing. Soon they were off to work at setting up their own projects, and Erin could tell Uncle Bub was thoroughly enjoying the scene. He kept looking about the huge room.

"Looking for more fans?" Erin asked, smiling at him as she began working to set up her project.

"What? Oh!—no, nobody in particular," he said, still looking in a distracted way. "There's just so much going on. By the way, your teacher will be here, won't she? You know, Miss Barbary?"

"Oh, yes—you may be sure of that!" Erin said. "She's more excited about it than anybody."

"Okay, let's get this show on the road!" Uncle Bub said, rubbing his hands together. "What's the schedule for today? I want to do whatever you need."

"Not much to do, really," Erin said. "We have the first hour to set up our science projects. Then we have to stand next to them while the judges come around to evaluate them. Then they name the three winners. After that, all the other teachers in the school bring their classes a few at a time to see our projects. This afternoon, it will be open to the general public, when everybody else. . . ."

"Whoops!" said Uncle Bub suddenly, interrupting her. "There she is! I see Miss Barbary! Be right back, Kiddo," and he was gone. Erin watched him cross to the other side of the room, where he and Miss Barbary shook hands. She watched them talking and then turned back to her project. It would be easy to set up, even without Uncle Bub's help. Not that it mattered, of course. She sensed that she wouldn't be seeing much of him this morning, not while Miss Barbary was around. She smiled to herself and got to work.

First she covered the table with a thick cloth colored deep green. That was her mom's idea. Then the huge colored atlas of the world which Uncle Bub found for her fit neatly on the wall behind her display, with the big arrow pointing to Belize. It would be clear to any and all who visited this display exactly where it fit into the world. Then the little covered cardboard stands, which she and her mother had made late one night out of cereal boxes, were placed at vantage points around the table to hold the charts and research reports on every aspect of the project: when the seed was found, the probable location in Belize, and all sorts of data on rainfall, sunshine, rain forests, with photos of the seed itself. It was probably more information than anybody ever wanted to know about this little-known area on the globe.

WHAT IS THIS PLANT? a big chart asked in bold letters. Below it were diagrams of the genus Bromelia and one for Digitalis, with question marks following characteristics of each one and what Professor Briscoe had been able to tell her from his study of the seed.

And then, right down front was the main attraction: the plant itself. Erin realized it didn't look like much—not much at all. It still sat there with its one big leaf and one little leaf, looking plain and undramatic. But, taken as a package, her display didn't look bad at all, she felt.

"I see you brought the flower-petal fabric," Uncle Bub said, just as she was finishing. "It looks perfect there. Good show!"

"It's an extra added attraction," Erin said. She had opened the fabric and draped it carefully over one edge of the pot holding the plant. That, too, had been her mom's idea, and it seemed to add just the right touch. She hoped that when the judges came by, they would ask her about it, because she felt it was somehow an important part of the point her project was trying to make.

Miss Barbary walked up. "Very good display, Erin," she said. "I'm making a final check of all the projects before the judges arrive, and I am so pleased with everything I see here today. You have all done so well with your projects. Some have even surprised me. This is going to be the best Science Fair we've had in years!"

"Guess I'd better be on my way before the judges get here," Uncle Bub said, glancing at his watch. "Your mom and I will see you this afternoon. Good luck, Kiddo!" and he soon disappeared in the crowd.

Slowly the other adults drifted out of the room, leaving only the students and their displays in the big room. Then came the cruising. The students, satisfied that their projects were set up and ready, began drifting around the room to check out what the other displays looked like. *Checking out the competition,* Erin told herself. She could see them bunched around certain displays here and there, but she decided to stay where she was. A number drifted by and offered nice comments about her project, but none really paused to read it. Erin knew that hers was the type of project that required some close examination, but she didn't know if that was good or bad. Either way, it didn't matter, she told herself. She was going to take her mom's advice: let the chips fall where they may.

Shortly, not to her surprise, Will Moreland sauntered by.

"Wow! It grew!" he said, springing over to the plant. "And what's this? It's beautiful!" He lifted one corner of the flower-petal fabic and then read the charts placed around the display. "Gee, this is really great," he said, his voice lower, and Erin could tell he was genuinely impressed—maybe not with the way it looked but with what it said. Somehow, that seemed important to her, and she appreciated him for knowing the difference.

"Thanks," she said. "More knowledge about an unknown plant than you'd ever want to know. But it was fun. Where's your project?"

Will pointed to the other end of the room. "Down there—oh, rats! The judges are here. Gotta go. Good luck!" he yelled, and took off.

Three more somber people Erin had never seen. Two women and a man, and all three wearing dark clothes, began moving like undertakers from one project to another, occasionally questioning a student here or there, but mostly talking in whispers to each other and not giving a clue as to their thinking. Eventually they arrived at Erin's display and stopped to peer at the charts and graphs and research reports. One actually went up to touch the plant and feel the flower-petal fabric, but said nothing.

Am I supposed to volunteer information? Erin asked herself, standing quietly next to her project. Miss Barbary had told them that the project had to speak for itself, but that they were to answer whatever questions the judges might ask. "But don't try giving them a sales talk," she had added. "Otherwise, they would never get around to all the projects." So Erin remained silent, her hands behind her back, and was relieved when they drifted on to the next project without saying a word. One, the older woman, looked at her and gave a fake smile as they passed by.

Then, almost before she knew it, it was over.

"Boys and girls," Miss Barbary announced in a loud voice from the middle of the room. "The judges have completed their rounds and have now handed me the names of the first, second, and third-place winners. Let's give a round of applause to our judges to express our appreciation for their wonderful help."

Thunderous and prolonged applause echoed in the large room from many pairs of sixth-grade hands grateful that the ordeal was over. The judges gave slight nods of their heads to acknowledge the applause.

"The white ribbon for third place goes to . . . ," and Miss Barbary paused dramatically. "Nancy Bazemore, for her project showing how Bonsai trees are grown and cultivated."

One of the judges strolled across the room and pinned the white ribbon on Nancy's project and shook her hand. Nancy smiled and clasped her hands together and couldn't restrain herself from doing two little jumps. Everybody applauded.

"The red ribbon for second place goes to . . ."

Miss Barbary said, "Will Moreland, for his display on the solar system."

Another judge walked over and pinned the red ribbon on Will's project, shook his hand, and led the applause for Will, who nodded his head, smiled, and managed a small wave to the crowd. Erin joined in the applause again but was a bit surprised. Will seemed almost shy in accepting the award.

"And the blue ribbon for this year's first-place winner of the Science Fair goes to . . ." Miss Barbary said with more fanfare in her voice than before, "Ralph Sims, for his display combining two of our most popular foods into one productive plant."

Ralph Sims yelled, "Yes!" and punched the air in front of him with a victory fist, and the applause broke

out spontaneously, with everyone laughing—except the judge, who soberly strolled over, pinned the blue ribbon on the display and shook Ralph's outstretched hand.

Miss Barbary held up her hand until things quieted back down.

``We want to congratulate our winners and thank all of our sixth graders for their hard work. Everyone learned something about science, and that makes every one of you a winner!,'' she said, and led yet another round of applause. ``Now, stand by your displays, because we are about to let the third graders in to see them. Answer all questions you may be asked. After that, we'll have fourth grade and fifth grade, and then after lunch the community will be allowed in. Keep your displays neat, now, and act like ambassadors for our school.''

She walked to the door with the three judges, shaking their hands all around, and a teacher marched in, followed by several gaggles of third graders. Erin took a deep breath. It was over. Over, at last. And nothing. She had won nothing. She glanced at her display. It still didn't look bad, she thought, but it would certainly look better with a ribbon on it.

Then she spied the flower-petal fabric. Maybe that's ribbon enough, she thought. Her feelings were all mixed up. She had wanted to win. All those hours and hours of work, all the frantic worrying, the moving the pot around, the research. But she was glad it was over, too. She just wasn't sure the chips had fallen where she wanted them to.

``Is that a dinosaur plant?'' a plaintive little voice asked, and Erin found herself surrounded by a small group of third graders. ``No,'' she said, and exhaled.

"It's a mystery plant. Nobody knows yet exactly what it is. But we're trying."

Maybe it was going to be an interesting morning, after all, she thought.

It went fast, and the afternoon went even faster. She answered lots of questions, especially from the fifth graders, who she figured were trying to prepare for their own Science Fair next year when they reached sixth grade. The adults had even more questions that afternoon. Erin still didn't know if that was good or bad, but she was too tired to care by the end of the day. Her mom and Uncle Bub returned, and Miss Barbary drifted about with them, looking at the various projects. Erin noticed that Miss Barbary was wearing a big tee-shirt over her blouse with a scene of the rain forest displayed in beautiful, brilliant colors on the front. On the back was "Jungle Love" in big green letters.

"Your Uncle David gave it to me," she told Erin when they reached her project again. "Isn't it gorgeous?"

This has been some day, Erin thought to herself as they strolled on past to see the adjoining projects.

Then Professor Briscoe came by with a small plastic bag and a tiny pair of scissors. "Now that we have a live specimen," he said, "I hope you will allow me to snip off just enough of one of these leaves for a cell study. I hate dead ends, and that's all I've found every time I try to identify this plant. May I?"

"Of course," Erin said, pulling the plant closer to the front. He carefully snipped a small piece off the side of the big leaf and the stem and dropped them into the plastic bag.

"And I'd like a few photos, if you don't mind. I'm

taking these to a Taxonomic Council meeting later this month in Paris and may find some expert help there from some of my colleagues. By the way, whose project was it that displayed the solar system?''

''Will Moreland's,'' Erin said, pointing across the room. ''There he is, talking to Miss Barbary and my Uncle David.'' She wondered what on earth the three of them could be talking about.

''Wonderful. I want to talk to him about my favorite theory concerning plants. Especially tumbleweeds.''

Will Moreland will love it, Erin thought, and found herself giggling inside.

While the professor took photos, Uncle Bub and Erin's mom came back to help her take down the charts and other displays to load into the car. They assured her that the project had been a success, even if she didn't win, and she was beginning to feel a bit better.

Then she looked up and saw Will Moreland standing there, and she wasn't so sure.

''You had the best project of all,'' he said, ''because it didn't have a cut-and-dried answer—sort of like outer space.''

For some reason, Erin felt he was telling the truth because of the tone of his voice.

''Thanks,'' she said. ''Sorry you didn't win first place.''

''Ah, I didn't really deserve it, anyway'' he said in an off-hand way. ''All I did was show what everybody already knows. That, and a lot of gimmicks. Mr. Oglethorp helped me with my special effects, or I probably wouldn't have even won second. Besides, who cares? It's over! We did it! We survived The Barb! Want to go to Nasty Ned's to celebrate?''

Erin was surprised.

"Nasty Ned's?'' she asked. It was a local eatery close to the school where mostly high school students went, with its big red sign outside that flashed *Nathaniel's Good Eats.*

"Sure,'' he said nonchalantly. "We'll order Good Gommy Gloppies.''

"Glood Glop. . . . what?'' Erin asked.

"Aha!'' Will almost shouted, pointing his finger at her and laughing. "That means you have to buy! It's the tradition! If you don't say it right the first time, you have to buy!''

Erin smiled in a twisted way. She was determined to try.

"Good . . . Gommy . . . Gloppies,'' she said slowly and evenly.

"Too late—you missed the first time! But since you didn't know—we'll share,'' he said.

"Let me ask my mom,'' Erin said, looking about.

"Already did,'' Will said, "And they said it's okay— both your mom and your Uncle David. He's a cool dude,'' Will said. "So's your mom. They were talking to my parents. We have to be home by five. A whole bunch of us are going, so we'd better be on our way.''

Far across the room, she saw her mom looking her way. Erin waved, and her mom waved goodbye. But she held up her arm and pointed to her watch, then held up five fingers. Erin smiled and nodded.

"Moms.'' Will said. "They're all alike.''

And they took off for Nasty Ned's, and Erin didn't feel like a loser at all.

Week of Wonders

It was a soft summer night, and the imperial moon slowly pulled up a shawl of fleecy clouds about its golden shoulders, much like the downy comfort that covered Erin as she lay sleeping in her room. As the clouds drifted silently across the balmy sky, they brought with them the softest of mists that filled the air and settled silently like glistening crystal dust on the landscape below. It was the kind of mist that swirled through the shimmering air on the gentle breezes of the night, curling here and there around corners and under the edges of things, seeping silently into every nook and cranny, beneath doors and under windowsills like the silky showers in the rain forests of Belize or the soft powdered sands of the desert where the tumbleweeds grew. It came without a sound, softly, like an untold secret.

In her bed, Erin's eyes fluttered. She was dreaming. In her dream, she was in a green glade, framed with plants in profusion, plants she had seen before and some she had not seen. Horace was there, and Claire and Thomas and Clementine and Pericles and all the others she knew, slowly waving in gracious movements back and forth, welcoming her to a strange new garden where other more mysterious plants grew, with blooms and blossoms and fronds and fragrances wonderful to behold.

Slowly the green glade shimmered into soft grey and disappeared as Erin awoke. Who knows what awakened her? Maybe it was the sense of the soft rain outside, the fragile touch of the change in temperature, the gentle hint of moisture from the mist. Slowly, she came to realize it was real. The scent she had smelled in her dream had come true; the fragrance was there all around her in her room. She sat up in bed. Strange. Maybe she was smelling some kind of exotic new perfume her mother had bought. Erin slipped out of bed and padded down the hall, but her mother was sleeping soundly in her room, and the fragrance seemed thinner in that part of the house. She went back, quietly searching for the source. It seemed to be getting stronger as she neared the sun room.

She clicked on the light and looked around. Over in one corner, nestled among her other plants where she had sensed that it seemed to like best, was the rain forest plant. And on a rich green stem between its two leaves was one of the most breath-takingly beautiful flowers she had ever seen. Lacy, dainty petals were in profusion, with the ruffled edges trimmed in deep violet, which faded gradually through many hues of purples and blues and finally ended in gleaming alabaster in the center. Entranced, she eased over to the flower and counted. There were seven petals, each curling up from the center and then cascading out in a gracious curve, and the fragrance lingered like magic in the air. She stood silently and without moving and looked at it for a long time. Then she smiled to herself, and, after a long while, clicked off the light and went back to bed.

Before she knew it, she felt her mother's quick peck on her forehead and the shades flaring open to let in a flood of muted light.

``Wake up, Kiddo! Almost time for me to leave for

the office. It rained during the night and it's still overcast this morning, so I let you sleep a little late," her mother said. On her way out, she paused. "So! My darling little girl is growing up and starting to wear perfume! What's the name of it? I love it! Whatever it is, you've *got* to let me use it! Did you borrow it from one of your friends? What a wonderful fragrance!"

Erin sprang out of bed, suddenly remembering, and rushed past her mom, heading for the sun room.

"It's not a perfume, Mom," she called back. "Come look!"

She rushed to the rain forest plant, with her mom following close behind. The petals of the flower had folded inward to make a small tight ball, with a deep green growth almost like velvet covering the outside. The smell was still there, but weaker.

"What an unusual looking thing," her mother said. "But anything that smells that wonderful is beautiful in my book. It's like smelling a rose for the very first time: nothing compares."

"You should have seen it last night," Erin said, and explained what she had seen.

"No wonder you slept late!" her mother said. "I certainly hope it blooms again tonight. Wake me up if it does. I want to see it. Do you think it will? Oh, that wonderful scent!"

Erin called Miss Barbary right after breakfast.

"Take pictures. Lots of pictures," her teacher said. "It has apparently made a seed, and we may have missed the chance to photograph the blossom. But take pictures of what it looks like right now, in case it doesn't bloom again tonight."

But it did bloom again that night. The deep green stem had grown beyond the first blossom and produced a second one—one that astounded Erin and her mother, not only because it was a different color from the first but also because the scent was different.

"Oh, that fragrance!" her mother exclaimed, as they stood there staring at the night-blooming plant. "Now I don't know which one I like better—last night's or tonight's. They're so different. Last night! Yes, that's my choice—last night's. No, tonight's. Definitely tonight's."

"Shhh, Mom," Erin hushed her. "Let's not make too much noise; we may disturb it. Just look."

The frilly edges of the petals on this second blossom were tipped in a deep bronze that slowly gave way to rich golden tones of burnished copper which in turn yielded to deep yellows and rich saffron before turning to a light green at the stem.

"Breathtaking," her mother said, a little more quietly this time. "You should call Miss Barbary again first thing in the morning and invite her over. She needs to see this for herself. And I'm calling your Uncle Bub as soon as I get to the office."

When morning came, Miss Barbary was there even before Erin's mom left for work. She studied the photos and the plant with intense excitement. The petals had closed in upon themselves like the first blossom and now seemed to be covered in a bright, shiny sheaf of blue silk.

"Absolutely fabulous!" Miss Barbary said breathlessly. "I have never—never—run across anything even remotely like this in the reference books. Each blossom is different and seems to make its own seed without dropping any petals. How totally impossible! I can't wait to call Professor Briscoe. Do you think your mom would mind if I bunked out here on your sofa tonight? I don't want to miss it if this wonderful plant does its thing again!"

And it did. The three of them stood there transfixed in the silence of the night, staring at the third blossom and inhaling its deep new fragrance.

"I am enraptured!" Miss Barbary said. "Surely the other two blossoms didn't smell as wonderful as this!"

"Oh, but they did, I assure you," Erin's mom said. "I just wish I could bottle all three. I think the first night is my favorite. No, the second. No, no—this one. Definitely this one."

"I brought extra film," Miss Barbary said. "Let's take as many pictures as we can, from every possible angle, without disturbing the plant."

The third blossom was fringed in a deep shade of garnet, which turned to lighter shades of rose and red and pink as it neared the stem. And, like the two before it, by morning its petals had slowly and methodically enfolded toward the center as if following some kind of silent, secret ritual that only Erin could stay awake long enough to watch.

"Please, please bring the flower to the lab," Professor Briscoe said the next morning when they called to tell him of the third blossom. "I have just received some exciting news myself to tell the two of you. And if your plant is doing what you say, it is imperative that I see it. I *must* see it!''

''That does it!'' Erin's mother said. ''No office for me today. This is getting exciting!''

They insisted that Erin hold it in her lap on the way to the lab. ''I wouldn't dare touch it,'' her mother said. ''Anything that looks and smells that good is bound to be very fragile and expensive, and I'd never forgive myself if I dropped it. I wonder if it likes coffee?'' She looked at Erin and laughed.

Erin smiled and rolled her eyes as she slid into the car seat with the plant in her arms. Miss Barbary drove with extreme care, Erin noticed, and avoided sudden stops and starts, as if they were carrying a priceless treasure that was easy to break. Erin wondered if they were.

The professor met them at the door of the science building and ushered them inside.

''We must make haste,'' he said, leading them quickly down the hall to the lab. Erin could tell that he was in a high state of excitement, and her pulse quickened, too. ''The most magnificent news! I have just received the final determination from a jury of my scientific colleagues, and they have confirmed what I suspected.'' He paused and looked at Erin. ''Remember the sample cuttings that I took from your plant back in the spring at the Science Fair? They showed cell structures and systemic properties that no one had ever recorded before. Your plant, young lady, is an undiscovered one. It makes big news in the science world when a new species is discovered. But we're talking about a new genus *and* a new species.

You have discovered a new plant, Miss Beddingfield! A completely new order of plant!''

"Oh, you haven't seen anything yet, Professor," Miss Barbary said. "Erin, let's show him the flowers and the photos. You won't believe it. You won't. Talk about new discovery!''

Erin found herself almost having to run to keep up with them. Finally they reached a section in the lab where a small platform was set up with a display table nearby.

"Place the plant there, please," the professor said to Erin, and began adjusting thin metal poles with lights on them at different angles around the plant. "I was so thrilled when I learned we had discovered a new plant that I prepared this area for a news conference. But then I received Miss Barbary's call this morning and think perhaps we should wait to see what transpires. Little did I dream that it may turn out to be so spectacular a discovery. May I see those photos?''

He took them from Erin's mom and looked at them very carefully, even the ones that seemed repetitious, and the only word he said was "Extraordinary." He said it so often that Erin thought she might begin counting how many times he used it.

"And you say the scent is different each night?" he finally asked, straightening up from his long inspection of the photos. "As different as the colors of each blossom?''

"So different you wouldn't believe," Miss Barbary said, "and absolutely fabulous. I realize that's not a very scientific word, professor, but that's what they are. Every one of them. Right, Erin?''

Erin was so awed by the seeming importance of all this that the only thing she could manage to do was smile and shake her head in agreement. Against such weighty talk by adults, she almost found herself blushing when they both paused and looked at her. But she didn't.

"Tonight we will hold another vigil," the professor said. "I must see for myself if this plant continues to perform in such an extraordinary fashion. And I must use night-vision film. No lights! We mustn't disturb the natural processes of the plant. Extraordinary!"

And so they did. And so did the plant. Erin's mother had brought blankets and pillows and snacks for them, and they bunked out in the lab, waiting and watching the plant. They were not disappointed. This time, from the first tiny movement of a petal unfurling to the last magic moment of its curling back tightly into another seed ball like the blooms before it, every step was videotaped in awestruck silence by the professor. And the scent, Erin and her mother and Miss Barbary assured him, was as stupendous as the others.

"I was never so frustrated," Erin's mother said. "Yesterday I was trying to describe how wonderful the smells were, and I realized that you can't describe a new fragrance. I guess that's why perfume companies are so free with their samples. How do you describe it? Especially anything as wonderful as these are!"

"Humm," the professor said, studying the stack of photos again as the first faint rays of light announced that a new day was dawning. Then he watched the videotaped segment of the newest bloom before turning once again to the photos. Sleepily, Erin and her mother and Miss Barbary peered at him through blinking eyes. What was he up to?

Finally he swung around in his chair and faced them. "We may look forward to three more blossoms, and no more," he said. "Miss Beddingfield, take a look at these photos and tell me why. You are the only one who would know for certain if I am correct."

Erin studied the photos from the first three nights. She saw what he was talking about almost instantly and wished she had thought of it before. Only she knew for sure, because only she had seen the first blossom the first night. And she remembered carefully counting exactly seven petals. The photos from the second night's blossom showed six, the third night five, and tonight's bloom had four. They had slowly opened in a graceful, even movement, like a slow-motion dance to unheard music, with two pointing up and two down. Their edges seemed to be glowing in a rich velvety green that almost matched the color of the stem, and from the edge the colors radiated down in slow gradations of green until a light blue emerged like a childhood memory of robin's eggs that turned to a light turquoise at the stem.

"You are right," Erin said, looking up at him. "Seven, six, five, four. . . ."

"What on earth are the two of you talking about?" her mother asked. "Is this some kind of countdown?"

"In a way, yes," the professor said. "I will ask my young colleague here to explain it," he added, taking off his glasses as he nodded toward Erin.

"The first night's blossom had seven petals," she explained. "I remember counting them. The one that bloomed the next night had six; you can count them in these photos. The third one had five. See? Here in this photo. And the one that just bloomed had only four. Unless we're wrong, tonight's blossom will have three petals, the next will have two, and the final one will have only one.''

''I cannot imagine the ultimate implications of this,'' Professor Briscoe said. ''How could anything—plant or animal—possibly evolve into this? It presents more questions than I could answer in ten lifetimes. Before we do anything, let's watch the full sequence of blossoms. Then we'll know for sure if we are correct. It is vitally important that we be correct.''

They were correct. The cavalcade of new blooms and scents continued that night and the next, each as entrancing and mystifying as those that had come before. The fifth night produced a three-petal display that was shaped like an ancient urn, with colors ranging from a burnt amber on the ruffled edge to a deep orange which faded to an unusual purple and then to a light orchid near the stem. The sixth night's two petals were tall and thin and elegant, like a piece of precious metal, but they were three distinct shades of white, beginning with an egg-shell white at the edges and gradually changing in hue to a pure, almost glowing white near the stem.

''Most extraordinary,'' Professor Briscoe muttered under his breath several times. ''Do you know that if you combine all the colors in the spectrum, what do you get? White! That's what! White, like this extraordinary flower before us, in three shades of white, yet. Most extraordinary!''

By the third day, he was clearly beside himself with excitement. Word had already leaked out about the fabulous new flower, and people were beginning to knock on the lab door, wanting to see it for themselves. Some came in small groups—garden clubs, civic organizations, flower societies, student groups, botanical associations, teachers—and others came as representatives of larger concerns, such as chemical companies wanting to manufacture perfumes with the new smells, or florists associations wanting to market the new plant for bouquets and gifts and arrangements, gardening companies wanting exclusive rights to sell the seeds, magazines wanting to buy color photos. The professor turned them all away, with a promise that the doors would be open tomorrow.

"We will have a news conference, right here in this lab," he told them. "Come back tomorrow at 3:00 o'clock." Then he turned to Erin and the others. "One night to go. The seventh night," he said calmly. "Can you imagine a flower blossom with one petal? What on earth could it look like? And what color could it be? We've already seen every color in the rainbow—the entire spectrum. I hope we won't be disappointed."

Late in the night, Erin was the only one awake. The others had nodded off hours earlier, wrapped in blankets scattered about the lab on tabletops and the floor. The professor was dozing in his chair. Just as she thought she detected a slight movement from the bud at the top of the plant, she heard the door on the far end of the lab open quietly, and a shaft of light from the hallway framed the figure of Uncle Bub. He held the door open and peered into the dark, trying to see. Finally, he spied Erin at the other end, outlined against the window in the soft light from a nearby exit sign. She waved, motioning him to her. He eased down the corridor between the tables and quietly squeezed her hand.

"Shhh," she held her finger to her lips. "You're just in time. Let's watch."

Sure enough, the bud had begun to open. She quickly woke the others, who rushed over. Professor Briscoe turned on the videotape. The bud slowly unfurled, and they beheld one single petal, a petal that unfolded like a piece of soft velvet that took the shape of an elegant little water pitcher, a petal that was the most exotic of all. At its tip it was coal black, and it changed hues to cobalt blue and ended in a silvery grey near the stem.

The professor sucked in his breath.

"The grand finale," he said, "and a most fitting one. Horticulturalists the world over have tried to cultivate a black flower for centuries. The concept of the absence of color in a flower has fascinated people for centuries. Great literature has been written about the romance and legend of the black rose, and every gardener in the world knows someone who knows someone else who is close to cultivating a black flower. But no one ever has. If you combine all the known color pigments, this is what you get: black."

"But . . . Professor," Erin hesitated to ask, but felt compelled to follow through. "Isn't that what you said about the white flower—if you combine all the colors, you get white?"

"Very good, Miss Beddingfield. Close, but not quite," the professor said, looking at her with a smile. "There is a difference, a most important difference. What I said was that you get white if all the colors of the *spectrum* are combined. You get black if all the *pigments* are combined. And that's what makes this plant so . . . well, so extraordinary. It has somehow managed in its processes to harness both the properties of light and of physical matter—the spectrum as well as color pigments. Forgive me, but I find this plant of yours to be absolutely. . . .''

''Extraordinary?'' Erin asked.

''Overwhelming, among other things,'' the professor chuckled. ''And I wish I were a young man again. There is a lifetime of answers to be studied, a world of discovery right here before us.''

They stood and stared silently at the blossom. Its scent, like the others before it, was alluring, enchanting.

''This has got to be my favorite. Absolutely. This is the best!'' Erin's mom said. ''If not this one, then the one that bloomed Tuesday. Definitely Tuesday—that's the one I like best. I think.''

Erin rolled her eyes and looked at Miss Barbary and Uncle Bub, who were standing side by side. They laughed.

''Thursday was my favorite,'' Miss Barbary said. ''Can you imagine what a company that makes perfume could do with these fragrances? All seven of them would be sensational! It would be worth millions and millions of dollars.''

''Everything about this plant is sensational,'' Professor Briscoe said, ''Its potential overwhelms me. So many unanswered questions. For instance, each blossom turns into a seed. If we plant that one seed, say the third, Wednesday's, for instance, would it then grow into a plant that contains all seven blossoms again? And would they follow the same order as this one when they bloom? Would they still smell the same? Oh—there are just too, too many questions. It's overwhelming.'' He shook his head slowly, almost sadly, and sighed. Then, he glanced at the black blossom again, and with renewed vigor, said to them, ''But we cannot keep this news any longer. Word is already out. There are many things to consider, many things that must be done. Go home,'' he told them all. ''Go home and get some rest, and come back this afternoon. I have alerted the news media. We must have a news conference. This will turn the international science world on its ear. People are already speculating. It's too important to hold back any longer.''

They waited until the black flower had curled its one elegant petal into a tight ball with a burnished golden coating on the outside, then they left. They were surprised to find little groups of people already gathered at the front of the building that early in the morning. The sun was just coming up. Several of the people ran up to them asking ''Professor Briscoe? Professor Briscoe?''

''No, he's still inside,'' Miss Barbary said. ''A news conference will be held this afternoon.''

Erin was amazed at the size of the crowd when they returned to the science building that afternoon. Every other person seemed to be holding a tape recorder or a television camera, and there were trucks parked nearby with the names of broadcasting companies in huge letters on the side. Cables and wires seemed to be everywhere.

They threaded their way through the crowd to the front. A roped-off area had been set up, with a podium that held a large assortment of microphones that bloomed like some kind of metallic blossom growing from a jungle of electronic stems. And there, standing down front, was Will Moreland.

"Wow!" he said, running up to Erin. "Can you believe this? Word is out that your rain forest plant has broken all the rules." He almost had to shout because the crowd was so large and everybody seemed to be talking excitedly at once.

Erin smiled. "No," she said. "It has just come up with a new set of rules. Trouble is, I don't think anybody knows what they are yet."

Will laughed. "But you'll find out, Beddingfield," he said. "I know you will. The professor told me his theory about plants and outer space. I think you may have one. Don't you think it may be from outer space?"

Erin was glad to see that he was smiling when he asked. Maybe he was growing up, too.

"Not from outer space," she said. "Inner space, maybe." He looked at her quizzically, and she added, "And it wouldn't surprise me if you turn out to be the world's first horticulturalist in space."

They were laughing together when the noise of the crowd subsided and there was a surge forward. The professor had entered from a side door and was approaching the podium. He stopped when he got to Erin, leaned over, and whispered in her ear.

"You must think of a name for the new plant," he said. Then he shuffled on past and stepped behind the podium. The reporters immediately began shouting questions. He held up his hands, waiting for the noise to subside again.

"Ladies and gentlemen," he said. "We are here to announce the discovery of a new plant—not just a new plant, but a new way of thinking about plants. . . .''

Cameras and tape recorders were whirring everywhere, and Erin listened as he explained the potential of the new plant and its strange new properties, the great possibilities its characteristics held for such fields as medicine, chemistry, genetics, agriculture, health, pharmaceuticals, horticulture, even art and commerce. Before he had gone very far, Erin was staggered at the great implications. She quietly eased to the side, away from the crowd, and watched from a distance. It was so much to think about. But she could handle it. She decided on a name for the new plant, a good one. Then, somehow feeling more confident than she had ever felt before, she placed her hands behind her back and listened from a distance as the professor continued.

''We are not even sure the seven seeds it has produced will ever grow,'' he said. ''In the rain forest, every living thing depends on some other living thing. Some flowers cannot survive without the help of particular insects, or a certain weather pattern, or even the presence of other plants. Who knows what kind of insect or other night creature these blossoms with their exotic scents must attract in order to survive? We do not know the origin of this plant; it has not been found growing in the wild, so we know nothing of its natural state. But we must find it in a hurry. Who knows? Its natural habitat may already be destroyed, and this one specimen may be the only one we will ever see. It will be treated like the treasure that it is. But we intend to search, and to keep searching until we find it—if it is there. We must!''

"What do you think the chances are, Professor?" a reporter asked. "How long do you think it will take?"

"The scientific community is already sending teams of researchers from all over the world," the professor said. "As for the chances, one can only guess. I like to think that, somewhere this very minute, in a small hidden glade in the rain forest, a plant just like this one grows, waiting for us to discover it and all the secrets it holds."

And I will be there to help find it, Erin said to herself. *This summer, or next year, or during the holidays. I will be there.*

"Professor," a reporter asked. "What is the name of this new plant?"

The professor smiled. "As you may know, it has long been the tradition in the science community that the discoverer has the honor of choosing a name. That's why we have plants and animals and countries—indeed, even comets and planets—named as they are."

Erin felt Will turn and give her a quick look, his mouth slightly ajar. He knew.

"In the same way," the professor continued, "the name of this new plant will go into all the international reference books and botanical journals because it has made history. To answer your question. . . ." he said, and paused, looking about the crowd until he spied Erin standing off alone to the side, framed by a large doorway. "You must ask the young lady whose diligence and care made it all possible. Ladies and gentlemen, Miss Erin Beddingfield!" he announced grandly, pointing to her. All faces turned to where she stood, and there was a brief pause. Then, like a wave that broke loose from a wall of water, the reporters turned and surged in her direction.

From where she stood in the doorway, Erin could see them coming, tripping over each other, tangling in the lines and wires, holding out microphones.

She smiled, and her smile, like the flower itself, was beautiful, filled with hope and promise.

ABOUT THE ILLUSTRATOR

Robert Ariail is the nationally award-winning editorial cartoonist for *The State* newspaper in Columbia, South Carolina. Two volumes of his collected cartoons have found wide audiences: the sold-out *Ariail View* and the more recent *Ariail Attack.* He is the winner of the 1992 Sigma Delta Chi Award for Editorial Cartoons and has also won the National Headliner Award. His illustrations are known widely for their humor, concise style and their outstanding concepts and execution.

ABOUT THE AUTHOR

Tom Parks holds a joint administrative/teaching appointment on the faculty at Clemson University. He is the author of over 200 articles, essays, short stories, plays, poems, and other written works appearing in local, state, and national publications. His series of editorial columns on teachers and teaching competed for the 1992 Pulitzer Prize in Journalism, and he currently serves as editor of three professional publications. He holds a Ph.D. degree in Applied English Linguistics from Peabody College of Vanderbilt University.